Jane McLoughlin, a great-great-great-niece of Sir Walter Scott, was brought up in rural England. She is a graduate of Trinity College, Dublin, and has worked as a journalist on the *Daily Telegraph*, the *Daily Mail* and the *Guardian*. She has written several non-fiction books and two previous novels. She now lives in Somerset in a seventeenth-century cottage, which she is busy restoring.

THE FURIES

A naked man is found dead on the mudflats near an English seaside town. If it is a simple case of drowning, what are the whiplash marks on the man's back? One young policeman suspects foul play by vigilantes and sets out to solve the mystery. But it is no mystery to the brutal Terry Naylor. He has been the victim of the Furies and he seeks revenge. Three women have little in common except a burning sense that the rule of law has let them down. Determined to see justice done, they take the law into their own hands. Unaware that both Naylor and the law are closing in on them, they plan one final act of vengeance . . .

JANE McLOUGHLIN

◆

THE FURIES

Complete and Unabridged

ULVERSCROFT
Leicester

First published in Great Britain in 2004 by
Robert Hale Limited
London

First Large Print Edition
published 2005
by arrangement with
Robert Hale Limited
London

The moral right of the author has been asserted

British Library CIP Data

McLoughlin, Jane
  The Furies.—Large print ed.—
  Ulverscroft large print series: thriller
  1. Vigilantes—England—Fiction
  2. Detective and mystery stories 3. Large type books
  I. Title
  823.9′14 [F]

  ISBN 1–84395–546–6

Prologue

'People like us don't do things like that,' Marjorie said.

'Who are people like us?' Clem asked.

'You know what I mean,' Marjorie said. She sounded defensive. 'Nice middle-class women, the sort of women old-fashioned gentlemen call ladies . . . '

'I'm not middle-class,' Clem said.

'We all are these days,' Marjorie said, 'you included.'

'I'm no lady,' Fiona said.

Marjorie didn't contradict Fiona.

'We did it before,' Fiona said.

'Yes,' Marjorie said, 'and it was dreadful.'

'Someone has to do something,' Fiona said. 'Someone's got to stop them.'

'I don't like it,' Marjorie said. 'I don't like it at all.'

'Well, you're in it now. It's too late to back out.'

Clem didn't say anything and her silence meant she agreed with Fiona.

'Tonight, then. We'll see to the second bastard tonight.'

1

He staggered as he came out into the cold night air. Then he stood by the harbour wall looking down on the dark water. Someone on one of the boats was playing a radio, a man was singing a song about a woman. A sad song. He'd never let any woman make him sad.

The only reason he drank in the pub by the harbour was because it was full of strangers. The summer visitors sat there under the striped umbrellas overlooking the water and none of them knew who he was or what he had done. In the pubs in the town centre there were more locals, and people moved away when he came in. He wore prison like an indelible mark setting him apart. But if there was a group of teenagers, even if there were girls, they crowded round him, they wanted to know what it had been like. Some of the girls touched him, putting their hands on his arm or leg, greatly daring as they asked him questions, as though he was an untamed lion and they expected he might bite.

He stood staring out across the water beyond the harbour wall towards the dark line of the headland. He saw the lights of a car swoop and curl. Lovers, he thought, looking for a place. He could imagine the girl. She would be eager. She wouldn't scream.

He needed another drink. People were coming out of the pub behind him, shouting 'Goodnight' to each other.

Then he became aware of a woman. She was standing a few yards away on the quayside smoking a cigarette. He could see the tip of it flare as she drew on it, and hear her slow breathing out of the smoke.

She moved towards him. She had dark glasses pushed up into her thick blonde hair. A street lamp cast a yellowish light on her. Her face was all shadows. She was wearing a short tight skirt.

'It's beautiful, isn't it?' she said.

He was startled that she spoke to him. He stepped towards her. She moved back, out of the light. Her face, behind the red point of the cigarette, was a blur.

He said, 'I wish I could offer you a drink.'

She threw the lighted cigarette into the water. He saw her face. She was young. No more than her early twenties.

'The pub's shut,' she said.

'Are you on holiday?'

'That's my boat. I came ashore to stretch my legs before we take her out.'

4

He became aware of the sound of a boat's engine ticking over in the dark under his feet. He moved closer to the edge of the quay. He could see lights from the cabin of a sailing boat.

'They don't like you tying up here since the marina opened,' he said.

'You can get a drink on board,' she said.

She told him her name, Tisiphone. 'You can say Tizzy for short,' she said.

She took his arm, directing him up the quay.

'There's the steps,' she said.

She leaned down to grip the top bar of the metal ladder set into the stone of the harbour wall. He resented the way she guided his hand to feel the iron rung. He had lived all his life in this town, he didn't need a jumped up little tramp tourist to tell him how to climb down to a boat. But she was offering him a drink. Her skin felt cool. He slid his hand up her arm. She didn't mind. She turned and smiled at him.

'Follow me down,' she said. He heard her land on the boat's deck below. 'Are you coming?' she called up to him. 'Come on if you're coming.'

He went down on his knees to grip the top bar of the ladder, feeling with one foot for a lower rung. He swung against the rough stone wall. A cold frond of wet seaweed curled round his neck. He slipped, missing a rung, his fingers sliding on the rusty metal as his arms took his weight. The boat tipped slightly in the water as he stepped on to the deck. The woman touched his hand. 'This way,' she said.

She was no more than a shadow ahead of him. He clung to the deckrail as he made his way aft towards the cockpit. The woman opened the hatch and shouted down the companionway.

'Ahoy, there. We've got company.' She had the sun glasses down over her eyes. In the light from the cabin below the skin of her bare arms looked silver. The metallic gleam against the dark sky behind her excited him.

She moved back to give him room to pass. He looked down into the cabin. There were two women there, sitting at the cabin table. They both wore masks. One was Minnie Mouse and the other was Mickey.

'What's this?' he asked. 'Fancy dress? Are you having a party?'

The woman with the Minnie Mouse mask wore shorts and had long, muscular, tanned legs; the one in the Mickey Mouse mask was older. She was a big, thick-set woman in a baggy sweater and jeans. They had their

6

smiling masks turned to him. They waved at him.

'Come on down,' the one in the Mickey Mouse mask said. 'You look like you could use a drink.'

The one in the Minnie mask pulled her long brown legs up onto the bunk on the right of the cabin and stretched them out in front of her.

'Hallo,' she said. Her voice sounded strange through the mask. She had lean muscular brown arms as well as strong legs.

'I'm Jim,' he said.

'Hallo Jim,' the leggy one lounging on the bunk said. 'I'm Alecto, but you can call me Ali.'

'And I'm Megaera, but it's easier to call me Meg,' said the older woman.

He smiled as if it was a great joke. 'Well,' he said, 'now we've been introduced.'

When people asked him who he was these days he often lied. Jim wasn't his name. They might have heard his real name.

'What will you have? Tequila?' the older woman said.

'Boy,' he said, 'tequila on top of what I've been drinking.' But he took it.

He wondered what they might have in mind bringing a man in there. It would be something to talk about if he had stumbled

7

into a lesbian scene.

The boat lurched. He staggered. The big woman pushed him down on to the bunk. 'Sit down,' she said. She gave him another drink. She had large hands, with big round fingers and short-cut nails. The reddish freckles on the backs of her hands extended up her broad fingers.

'Down the hatch, Jim,' the one with the legs said. She sat beside him, stretching her legs across the cabin-well under the table.

The blonde from the quayside put her head through the hatchway. He thought she looked silly wearing dark glasses at night, like a film star trying not to be recognized. He felt nervous. He wished they'd show themselves and act normal.

'We're off, then,' the blonde said.

'Off?' he said. 'What d'you mean, off? Where are we going?'

The big woman ignored him. The one with the legs turned her Minnie Mouse mask at him and shrugged.

'I don't care,' he said. 'I got nowhere to go. You can sail me to France for all I care.' He drank the rest of his drink and the big woman brought him another.

The engine note altered, became louder and faster like a recording of the heartbeat of an athlete starting to run fast. A faint smell of hot diesel filled the cabin. The boat swung away from the quay and water hissed under the hull as they began to move across the harbour.

He could see the stars through the open hatch. A pinprick of light moving laboriously across the sky was an aircraft. He took another drink from the big woman.

At one point, both the women went on deck. He slid sideways on the bunk. The loud clatter of an anchor chain aroused him at last. He tried to jump up. He was confused. He banged his head against a grab rail on the bulkhead. 'I'm drunk,' he said aloud.

The boat began to roll and pitch in the swell. He fell back heavily. He felt sick. They came down the companionway, the two still in the silly grinning masks, the little blonde still wearing her dark glasses.

'Well, Martin, are you enjoying the trip?' she asked. All three had their heads turned towards him, looking down at him.

'Hey,' he said. He tried to move but his legs wouldn't function. He seemed to have lost control of his face, too. It was like trying to speak after an injection at the dentist. 'How do you know I'm Martin?' he tried to say. But it didn't sound like that.

The one with the long legs, who had been so cheery, grabbed the collar of his shirt. He heard the cotton rip and a button break off. The big one held his arms pinioned. He couldn't move.

'Hey, what's this?' he tried to say.

The one in the Minnie Mouse mask held his arms behind his back. He couldn't pull himself free. His arms felt as if they were filled with straw.

The big one bent and grabbed his ankles. He tried to kick her, but he couldn't move his legs.

He tried to say, 'No, please, no,' but the words didn't come out. They had his jeans down over his knees.

The little blonde put her hands between his legs and squeezed. 'Not much there,' she said. 'You wouldn't think he could cause such trouble with that little thing.'

He tried to speak.

'What?' she said. 'What did you say?'

'What do you want with me?' he said. 'Who are you?'

They pulled off his trainers, then dragged his jeans over his bare feet. Then they hauled him up the companionway into the cockpit by his arms. He tried to kick but all the strength had gone out of his legs. Two of them, the big woman and the tall athletic one, pulled his arms over the boom, holding his wrists down so that he hung there with his cheek pressed against the cold canvas of the stowed sail. Then the little blonde stepped up to him. The one with the long legs grabbed a handful of his hair and pulled his head back so that he had to look up. The little blonde had a whip in her hand. It was a big whip with a long lash like the ones animal trainers used in the circus.

'For God's sake!' he said. His voice was thin and shrill, hysterical like a whistle. 'Stop it,' he said.

'Did you stop when she screamed?' the one in the Minnie Mouse mask asked. 'She begged you to stop, didn't she?'

'You didn't show her any mercy, did you?' the big one said. 'No mercy whatsoever. Do as you would be done by, Martin.'

'You ruined that girl's life,' the one in the Minnie Mouse mask said.

'You did rape her, didn't you?' the big one in the Mickey Mouse mask said.

'And then you beat her up,' the blonde said. 'And now I'm going to beat the shit out of you.'

He was very frightened now, shivering. That girl they were talking about had made him angry. To start with, he'd treated her like a kid sister, given her a friendly warning that she was asking for trouble dressed like that. She'd got into his car. She'd been begging for

11

it. Even that journalist Barry Pearson said she was begging for it, dressed the way she was, getting into a stranger's car in the middle of the night, making up to him. How was he to know she was only thirteen?

He felt angry now at the memory of that little tramp pushing him away when he tried to kiss her. She'd been asking for it, but she wouldn't even let him kiss her once in a nice way. She got what she deserved. He'd done her a favour, giving her a lift, and she wouldn't even give him a little kiss.

The little blonde brought the lash down across his naked back.

He wanted to say something but he only screamed.

'Listen,' the big woman said, 'we don't like rape. We think rapists need a dose of their own medicine. You can see the logic of that, can't you? It's only justice after all, that you should have some idea what it's like.'

'Yes,' the one in the Minnie Mouse mask said, 'you'll get justice here, this isn't a court of law.'

He opened his mouth to speak but nothing came. 'No one would hear you,' Mickey Mouse said. 'There's no one to hear you, the same as there was no one to hear her.'

The blonde lashed him again. He cried out. He had never felt pain like that in his entire life. He jerked himself upright, screaming. He tore his hands free of their grip and scrambled across the cockpit. Then he flung himself over the stern rail into the cold black water.

2

Marjorie Warren used to be known to her friends as the 'Pillar of Salthaven'. It was an acknowledgement of all the sandwiches she'd made to sustain her husband Ben's political supporters; all the jumble she had sold; all the smiles she had given strangers as his consort on council business: but the nickname, Marjorie knew, was never affectionate. She'd never really existed for other people except as Ben's wife, mother to Peter and Tessa.

That had been enough for her. She'd always known exactly who and what she was. She'd been happy, or, at least, content.

It wasn't even the breakdown of her marriage that ended her cosy world. When Ben told her he was in love with someone else, she'd understood. She would turn a blind eye. That hadn't been enough; he wanted a divorce. Ben was a public figure and couldn't get away with leaving her. She had to be in the wrong. So because she loved Ben, she'd let him blame her and he married Nathalie. And he'd done the decent thing by buying a nice Victorian semi-detached villa on the outskirts of town for his discarded

14

family, Marjorie, Peter and Tessa.

Marjorie had even come to terms with Peter leaving home to live in Australia. Peter blamed Marjorie for the break up. Marjorie resented that. She thought he ought to have worked out that Ben was the one who'd had someone else to marry. In any case, Peter never wrote or called. For a while, he'd kept in contact with his sister, but there had been nothing since Tessa disappeared.

That was what had destroyed everything. 'I was more or less sane,' Marjorie said aloud to herself, 'until Tessa disappeared.'

It was a morning just like this, rain drumming against the conservatory and cloud blotting out the view of distant hills. Tessa had been out to a disco the night before with friends from the building society where she worked. Marjorie let her sleep in. At noon, though, she'd taken Tessa a cup of tea upstairs to wake her and found that her daughter's bed hadn't been slept in. Marjorie never saw Tessa again.

That was ten months and twenty days ago: ten months and twenty days of not knowing if Tessa were alive or dead; of long nights of black despair punctuated by glorious night-mares which seemed so much more real than the bleak reality of being awake. Marjorie dreamed that Tessa was walking in the door, calling 'I'm home'. And she'd wake up believing that the dream was true, until her own joyous, empty, calling of her daughter's name brought her back to painful real life.

When Tessa disappeared, Marjorie was destroyed. Outwardly, nothing much changed, but inside the big, motherly façade, she was broken into tiny pieces. And it got worse as time went by. That was the horrible thing, to Marjorie. She expected time to heal, but it didn't. She found she had an infinite capacity to give herself reasons for hope. And there was the painful, burning anger she could not give vent to because not knowing what had happened gave her no one to blame. The anger built up inside her.

That's what Clem and Fiona and I have in common, Marjorie thought, we're all crazed.

What's happened to me? she thought. That boy might be dead. Some other woman may be going through what I suffered when I found Tessa missing.

Marjorie had to get out of the house, away from the rain and the silent bedroom upstairs and the endless emptiness echoing to the sound of that young man's scream and the sound as he jumped and his body hit the water. Then there'd been silence. They'd searched for hours, but there was no further sound except the murmur of the wind in the rigging.

She knew where the others would be, and why. Clem and Fiona would be in the gym, trying to use physical effort to keep a memory at bay. In one way or another they'd all three of them been doing that since they first met there. It was what brought them together in the first place. They still did it.

The Fitness Centre was in the basement of a converted warehouse in the docks area of the Old Town. Marjorie parked her ageing Deux Chevaux in the multi-storey car-park opposite and hurried into the club.

The girls on the treadmills looked up at Marjorie without seeming to see her. Marjorie thought, is that how Tessa saw me? An irrelevance? Did she feel smothered and run away from me? Oh, no, no, no. Even the police had finally assumed Tessa was murdered. There was a full-scale murder hunt, but then they seemed to have given up looking for her or her killer. Only Tom Wheeler, the local bigwig, had made any kind of fuss when they gave up searching for Tessa. Marjorie was bitter. She was angry with those smug-sounding policemen. They droned on at her, they were doing all they could, they offered her counselling. If they had anything of any significance to say they talked to Ben

17

instead of her, and when they spoke to him they spoke as equals, whereas if she forced them to speak to her, they treated her as though they were chiding a fractious child instead of communicating with a woman being driven crazy, without even her daughter's body to lay to rest.

Clem was finishing a circuit in the gym. She hurried across to Marjorie.

'Thank God you've come,' she said. 'Is there any news?'

Marjorie shook her head. 'We need to talk,' she said. She felt like a conspirator. She was a conspirator.

'Fiona's in the salad bar,' Clem said. 'I'll come with you.'

Fiona was alone in the bar. It was a quiet time, and the staff were taking a break. She was dressed for the office. She looked out of place here. The walls were hung with enlarged photographs of robust, all but naked, men and women in muscular poses. Marjorie thought Fiona looked too thin, all knobbed bones like an exotic bright little stick insect, sitting there under those pictures. Marjorie thought she didn't look real. She looks more real when she's wearing that blonde wig, she said to herself, at least she looks like a real person in disguise then.

She wished Fiona wasn't there, even

though she knew the three of them needed to decide together about what they must do. Marjorie wanted to discuss it with Clem first, to talk through what had happened, talk about it so much that it wouldn't be real any more. That wasn't possible with Fiona. With Fiona, there was no opportunity for obscuring reality, not even the chance to get used to an idea. Fiona confused Marjorie, but there was something about her, a vitality, that was magnetic. Fiona wasn't like any other woman Marjorie had ever met. Fiona didn't seem to *feel* anything; she simply got a funny look in her eye and it was as if she cast a spell over people. When Marjorie went home, when Fiona wasn't there anymore, she wondered why she let Fiona dominate her. It was like being hypnotized, she decided. Fiona did it to Clem, too, and Clem seemed happy to go along with it. But it frightened Marjorie.

She and Clem sat down at Fiona's table. Marjorie glanced at the mobile telephone on the table in front of Fiona. 'Has there been any news?' she asked. Fiona shrugged and shook her head.

Marjorie said, 'Suppose it all comes out?' She sounded as though she were pleading with Fiona to give some sign that she was frightened too. At the same time, the young woman's lack of fear comforted her.

'Why should it?' Fiona said.

'He's dead,' Marjorie said. 'He's probably dead.'

'So he can't talk,' Fiona said. 'If he drowned, he drowned. Why should anyone ask questions? Everyone will think he had a guilty conscience. He should've had. No one's going to connect us with anything.'

'Is that it?' Clem said. 'Is that all it means to you?'

'What do you want, remorse?' Fiona said. Her voice sounded harsh. 'You of all people?'

'It's different. We didn't kill Naylor.'

'We didn't kill this one,' Fiona said. 'He killed himself.'

She looked from Clem to Marjorie. 'Neither of you objected to doing what we did to Terry Naylor,' she said. 'This wasn't any different.'

Marjorie said, 'It is different this time. Terry Naylor didn't die. This boy may have died.'

'Too bad Naylor didn't die,' Fiona said.

Naylor was the first rapist they'd taken care of. They did it for Clem. Naylor was the one who raped Clem, but her uncorroborated identification hadn't been enough. He'd got away with it. She'd left the court branded at least a liar. Many saw Naylor as the victim. Several newspapers hinted that she was a vindictive woman scorned. Fiona and Marjorie, though, had no doubts. They'd wanted to give her proof positive that they believed her. She'd been in a bad way, and they knew she needed action, not words. So they'd hoped that if they executed a measure of justice themselves, she might be able to move on in her life.

It had been Fiona's idea. Fiona's previous boss had taken his family on a two-year secondment in Africa and left her in charge of his yacht, the *Eumenides*. One night, she and Clem and Marjorie were on board together. They were waiting for the tide to take the boat out. Clem asked about the name, and Marjorie explained about the Furies of Greek myth. She knew their names: Tisiphone, Alecto, and Megaera. It had started almost as a joke, the three of them as modern avengers of women let down by justice. Fiona was Tizzy; Clem, Ali; Marjorie was Meg. And then it had seemed like a good idea to avenge Clem.

Naylor had broken into Clem's room in the university hall of residence in the early hours of a morning and raped her. She'd woken up to find this man in a balaclava holding a knife to her throat. She tried to fight him off, and ripped off the balaclava. She'd seen his face. The only light had been the dim reflection of a street light outside the window, but she'd seen enough to recognize him. He'd stabbed her and left her for dead.

Clem picked Naylor out of the police files. She had no doubt. Then, in court, the judge ruled that her identification alone wasn't enough. The victim had been in a bemused state, in the dark, how could she be certain? He dismissed the case.

That's why the three of them had done what they did.

Perhaps they were all thinking of that when Fiona said she wished Naylor had died. There was a pause. Then Clem tried to speak, but Fiona went on, 'I know, with Naylor we were redressing injustice. It wasn't revenge. That's what we agreed, we kept it impersonal. Well, this time it wasn't one of us who was the victim, but what happened was just as bad. That poor kid who killed herself didn't get justice either. Martin Bakewell deserved to be punished. It wasn't our fault the moron jumped overboard.'

Clem said, 'It was personal, with Naylor. For me it was. I can't help it, I wanted revenge, whatever I said. So this is different. I only agreed because you'd helped me with Naylor and I felt guilty that I might not be unselfish enough to do it for someone else. But killing him . . . ' She sounded doubtful.

'It was an accident. He'll just be another drunk who took his clothes off for a sobering swim and drowned,' Fiona said.

Marjorie said, 'What kind of drunk flagellates himself with a whip? You must've marked him.'

Fiona's eyes were very bright. It's as though she's high on something, Marjorie thought. She was excited like that with Naylor.

Fiona laughed. She asked, 'So what's your plan? We go and confess to murdering a young man who may not even be dead?' She ignored the No Smoking sign and lit a cigarette.

'You can't smoke in here,' Clem said.

'No one's going to know.'

'I work here, remember?'

'It's illegal,' Marjorie said.

'No, it isn't,' Fiona said. 'There's no law against it, it's just a fascist bureaucratic regulation.'

'I wasn't talking about smoking,' Marjorie said. 'I meant what we did.'

'Legal, illegal,' Fiona said, 'where did legality ever get anyone?'

'You just hate men,' Marjorie said.

Clem asked, 'What happened to you, Fiona? I was raped and Marjorie's daughter was murdered — '

'We don't know that,' Marjorie said. She could feel heat rising in her face and struggled to stay calm. 'Tessa may still be alive.'

For a moment Fiona seemed about to tell Marjorie that her determined optimism was ridiculous, but she saw Marjorie's face and said nothing.

'So, Fiona?' Clem insisted.

Fiona shrugged. 'Oh, you know, the usual thing. First my father, when I was a real kid. I was eight when he left and my uncle started. Then it was my mother's boyfriends. I wonder what kind of woman she really was, she seems to've been addicted to child abusers.'

Marjorie thought, she *sounds* as though she's talking about someone else, but can she really *feel* like that?

'That's awful,' Clem said.

Fiona said, 'Of course, I never liked playing second fiddle, not even to my mother.' She smiled.

Marjorie thought, is she trying to make a joke of it? She had a vision of Fiona's mother in a Laura Ashley skirt, a long-haired hippie, a woman who had come of age in the seventies and was probably still floating through life in a camper van talking of peace and love. If she hadn't died of a drug overdose, of course. Marjorie found it hard to believe that Fiona had had any kind of mother; she'd never mentioned her before.

'Oh, for Christ's sake, Clem, wipe that sympathetic look off your face,' Fiona said. 'Actually, I liked it, usually. But all that was years ago.'

She's crazy as hell, Marjorie thought. But in spite of herself she felt envious at the way Fiona had been able to put things behind her. The young woman had made something of herself. She was only in her early twenties, about the same age as Tessa when she disappeared, but she had everything, an executive job, a smart flat, a yacht.

There was a sudden clatter and sound of laughter from the kitchen. The catering staff were coming back on duty after their break. Fiona stubbed out her cigarette in a saucer. She picked up the mobile telephone and put it in her bag. 'I've got to go,' she said, 'I'm late for work.'

She got up to leave. 'What's done is done,' she said. 'The question is, where do we go from here?'

3

Detective Constable Hobbs looked down at the staring blue eyes. He had to look away. The constable was young and he had not seen many corpses since leaving traffic duty, and he had not liked seeing those either.

Dr Walsh, a fat man, was squatting painfully beside the body. Hobbs thought Dr Walsh with his large glasses looked like a bullfrog among the reeds. The dead man was stretched out on the shining mud naked as a fish.

'How long?' Hobbs asked him.

'Only hours,' Dr Walsh said. 'Not more than twelve. That's only a rough guess.'

The body had been washed up on the mudflats at the mouth of the river. It was a lonely place, protected from the open sea by the headland behind Salthaven. Birdwatchers came here, but although it was close to the town in a direct line, the only road took tourists several miles inland to cross the promontory.

A man exercising a Labrador had found the body. Or, rather, the dog had found it. The elderly man and his dog were still there. The man was an old boy in a tweed coat. He was shocked and nervous.

Hobbs went over to him. He offered him a cigarette and gave him a light. He did not light up himself. He didn't smoke. He carried them to soothe other people's nerves.

'Nothing I could do,' the man said. 'I didn't know what it was at first. I heard the dog yelping. He knew he'd found something unusual. You know how they do? I ran back to the cottage and told my wife to ring you lot, then I came back. I couldn't find any clothes, you know, his clothes.' He gave a quick, embarrassed look at the nakedness of the corpse. 'Look at that mud. You'd think him being in the water he'd be clean. What could I do?' He was appealing to Hobbs for some sort of comfort.

Hobbs said, 'You go back home now, sir. I'll be along later.'

The man looked doubtful. He seemed to think Hobbs was cheating him out of the importance of his role.

'Nasty shock,' Hobbs said, 'finding him like this. Not what you expect.'

The man nodded. He called his dog. Hobbs watched them make off through the reeds towards a small whitewashed cottage across the marshes. Bleak bloody place, Hobbs thought. In the winter it must be like living on the moon.

Oddly enough, the body did not look out of place here. Waxen, stiff, it could easily have been one of the half-fossilized pieces of wood lying among the reeds, bleached by salt and sun, half-buried in mud.

The tide was coming in. The water washed round the doctor's rubber boots and round the corpse.

'Drowned. No doubt about it,' the doctor said. He took out a handkerchief to wipe his hands.

Hobbs turned and looked across the estuary at the reeds bending in the mud like flattened hair. Away to the right, crowds of sea birds gathered on the mud flats at the water's edge. The waves broke gently there, lapping the long legs of waders. Further out, the current drew swirling patterns on the grey water where the river channel flowed into the sea.

'I wonder who he is?' Hobbs said.

'No way of telling. No distinguishing marks I can see. Except these.' Dr Walsh pointed at the man's back.

'What?' Hobbs did not want to look closely at the corpse.

'These wounds.' Dr Walsh leaned forward and prodded the corpse with his foot, rolling it slightly sideways. Hobbs could see marks on the man's back. 'Can't tell yet,' the doctor said. 'I may know more when I've got him cleaned up on the slab.'

'Suicide?' Hobbs said.

'He drowned.'

'An accident?'

'I suppose if you swim about naked in the middle of the night, accidents do happen. Perhaps he was drunk.'

'Well,' Hobbs said, 'those are marks of violence.'

'They're not fatal,' Dr Walsh said. He looked down at the body. The body was tanned except for the strip of white skin across the buttocks and the blueish weals across the back and shoulders. 'He could have done them himself,' Dr Walsh said, 'or got a friend to do them.' Dr Walsh was a cynic. He looked at Hobbs to see if he appreciated his humour. Hobbs didn't. 'I'll let you know as soon as I can,' the doctor said. 'You'll get my report.'

He turned away. The mud tugged at his boots as he walked and he moved slowly. Hobbs watched the doctor making his way through the reeds back to the cars and the ambulance parked on the road. The road was a track. It ran from a village, hidden behind the headland, to the cottage where the old boy who found the body lived. Behind the

29

group carrying the body on a stretcher, the mud flats were now under water. The birds had flown away. As the men pushed their way through the reeds to the road their footprints were wiped clean behind them by the rising tide.

Hobbs waited until the body had been taken away and the uniformed men had left in their cars. He walked along the shore to the bleak cottage to take the old man's statement.

Driving back to the station, he decided to drop in at home. He wanted to change his wet shoes and put on dry socks.

He lived with his married sister, Sonia, and her husband, Gavin, on one of the new private housing estates on the outskirts of Salthaven. Gavin was the manager of a shoe shop in the centre of town. Sonia had recently returned to part-time work. She spent three afternoons a week in Salthaven working at a support group for the victims of rape and violence.

Hobbs liked the new red-brick house with its diamond-paned windows and the good big garage with a bench where he could do his woodwork. He liked the way the houses were all the same; the continuity gave an impression of being solid and respectable. He liked living with Sonia and Gavin. He had tried sharing a flat with a colleague from work, but he had not enjoyed it. With Sonia and Gavin he was part of a family and he felt at home.

Sonia was loading the washing-machine as he came into the kitchen. She was short and plump but had a pretty face. She smiled, surprised to see him.

'Bill, what are you doing here this time of day? Don't tell me you've actually got those figures for me?'

She wanted Hobbs to use the police computer to get her some figures on rape. She was going to give a talk to the Townswomen's Guild about her support group.

'I'll do it today,' he said. 'When they're all at the pub I'll play with the computer for you.'

His shoes had left a muddy track across the floor. 'Sorry,' he said.

'Where've you been, for God's sake?'

Hobbs took off his sodden socks.

'A body washed up on the marshes,' he said. 'On the estuary.'

'What kind of body?'

'Young man. Drowned.'

'Poor bastard.'

She spoke with a soft local accent. She made the word sound affectionate.

31

She picked up his wet socks. She held them at arm's length, then dropped them into the empty clothes basket.

Hobbs thought how bright the kitchen was, bright and cheerful. 'Time I got back,' he said.

'Are you in for dinner?'

'Hope so,' Hobbs said. 'I'll let you know if not.'

Sonia gave him a humorous look. She tried to make a joke of it, but it was a sore point between them that Hobbs had a woman now, and she was a married woman.

Hobbs was thinking about Annie as he drove back to work. He hoped she had not been ringing him at the station while he was out. He'd often told her not to, but she kept doing it. He was going to have to do something about Annie.

At the station Dr Walsh called.

'You'll get my report,' he said, 'but I thought I'd let you know before.'

'Don't tell me he didn't drown?'

'Oh, he drowned all right. But those marks, they were lashes from a whip. Quite nasty, as a matter of fact. A degree of malice behind those, I'd say.'

'How would he get them?' Hobbs said.

'Oh,' Dr Walsh said, 'probably some kind of weird sex. I wouldn't know about that. There was no sign of recent sexual activity. But there are bruises on his wrists. He'd been held down.'

'Why?' Hobbs asked.

The doctor laughed. 'To stop him fidgeting?' he said. He was laughing at Hobbs's innocence. He went on, musing, 'You tell me, you're the detective.' Dr Walsh sounded like Sonia.

Hobbs had much to do but he found it hard to concentrate. He had to go out that afternoon and did not finish until nearly six o'clock. Normally he would have driven straight home and then gone round to see Annie. Instead he went back to the police station. He'd promised Sonia those statistics.

Then Detective Sergeant Howard came in and asked what he was doing. Hobbs said he was just finishing writing up his notes.

'That body on the mudflats,' Hobbs said, 'he'd been whipped.'

'Don't get carried away,' Sergeant Howard said. 'Just clear things up as fast as you can. A drowning's a drowning. Nothing special at sea.' Sergeant Howard's father had a boatyard. Sergeant Howard was full of stories about the mystery of the sea but he never went near the water if he could help it. 'We'll be in the pub,' he said.

When Sergeant Howard was safely out of

the way, Hobbs sat down at the computer to get the information Sonia wanted. He began to call up available information on rapists and rape cases in the district over the previous five years.

Hobbs sat staring at the screen as the catalogue of case histories scrolled down. Most files had pictures attached. When the time came, he thought, he would not let a daughter of his go out with any men who looked like these. But then, they all looked so ordinary. You couldn't tell.

Hobbs leaned forward and continued his search among the dark lives that flickered across his screen. A young man's face appeared. Here was another one who didn't look like Hobbs' idea of a rapist. He was a pleasant-looking young man, or he would have been in a different context. Hobbs had seen him before, just that morning, stretched out in the mud, very dead, and not at all pleasant to look at.

4

Fiona lived in a flat on the first floor of a converted Edwardian house halfway up the steep slope of the headland above the harbour. She had lived there now for nearly two years, the longest time she'd spent in one place. The flat was like a film set. A bay window looked across the tops of Cedars of Lebanon to the sea. Trees and shrubs blocked the sight of neighbouring houses, and hid the ugly sprawl of the town, but at night she could see the lights of Salthaven, her private Impressionist painting.

Often, when she was out at sea, Fiona would sweep the headland with her binoculars to catch sight of her big bay window. Sometimes, sailing back in the early evening, the sun reflecting on the glass of the window made it look as though there was someone in the room. The first time that happened she was frightened and she stayed the night on the boat, afraid to go home and open the door of the flat in the dark in case someone was there.

Looking out of that window now she saw on the horizon the slow-moving hull of an oil tanker in the shipping lanes. The ship disappeared for a moment behind Studholme, a small island off the western headland of Salthaven Bay. She paused, standing in the quiet, bright room, watching the rolling white horses on the grey sea. In spite of herself she could not keep from thinking of the young man who had jumped overboard. Then she thought of Terry Naylor whom they'd left whimpering on the beach. Naylor had got an erection when she whipped him, even if Marjorie had tried to pretend afterwards that she hadn't seen any such thing.

They had paid Naylor back for raping Clem. And that's all they'd had in mind for last night's idiot. It had been Fiona's own idea. She was the one who'd got the others going. Fiona wondered why she couldn't identify with victims like Clem and the young girl who'd committed suicide. She felt she had something missing in her psyche, except that she thought it wasn't a lack in her, but a strength. She was different from most other women. Deep inside, Fiona felt she understood the feelings of Naylor and of the young rapist who had jumped overboard. She knew what they both must have felt when faced with their victims' abject fear. Not exactly contempt, not anger nor lust, but a kind of loathing which embraced the weakness of both the victims and themselves. They would have gloried in their power. She felt powerful like that when she whipped them and they could not hide their fear, when they pleaded with her to let them go. Fiona had often fantasized about Terry Naylor, seeing him in bed with an erection dreaming of her coming at him with the whip.

Fiona had come home to listen to the local television news. A body should have turned up by now, if there was a body. She'd told her boss she needed to go home to change. Today was important: Tom Wheeler, the man the newspapers said had the Prime Minister's ear on everything industrial, was visiting her company to look at a new computer security system. If he bought it, according to Frank Borden, the chief executive, the future was assured. Fiona had the job of persuading Tom Wheeler.

It was time for the local news summary. Fiona turned on the television. Nothing about a drowned man. She was relieved. She turned off the television and stood in the bay window watching the wind race across the tops of the trees.

If he's alive he won't talk, she told herself, it would be too shaming for him to admit what happened. If he's drowned, though, she thought, his body will turn up. But, dead or alive, why should they connect him with her? She'd been wearing the blonde wig when she picked him up; if anyone had seen her last night in the dark, they wouldn't recognize her again.

Fiona smiled, thinking of the judge who let Terry Naylor go because Clem hadn't seen her attacker in the light of day. The law was moronic. But if they found a body, the police might check who might have been sailing last night. The nightwatchman at the marina could have noticed her going, or coming back. But boozy old Ted was probably skiving off at the pub when they took the *Eumenides* out. With any luck the old drunk would have been sleeping it off when they returned in the early hours. Fiona began to imagine the police closing in. Marjorie and Clem would be hopeless. They couldn't lie to save their lives. Their lives weren't that wonderful to bother saving, perhaps, but she had a lot to lose. My trouble, she thought, is I've too much imagination, and that's a hangover from Rose.

Rose was her mother. Fiona remembered her as a silly woman with a shrill little voice who drifted from one man to another, alcoholic to drug addict to schizophrenic, without a thought of what would happen next. Rose had always insisted that she was a free spirit. Free? When she was always at the beck and call of chance and circumstance. It could've been so different; Rose didn't have to struggle to survive. Her parents had left her money, a lot of money. But she'd spent it; wasted it; gave it away.

Rose hadn't wanted Fiona filled with a lot of false notions, so she kept her away from school and pretended to teach her at home among the joss sticks and last night's wine bottles. Fiona had got herself pregnant at fourteen, but she hadn't told Rose. She knew that Rose would've wanted her to keep the kid and they'd live hand to mouth but *free*, raising the child together. Even if Rose had guessed its father was her own boyfriend, she was so stupid she'd probably have been pleased. She'd have said it made them a real family.

That wasn't what Fiona wanted. By the time she realized what was wrong with her, it had been too late for an abortion. All that free love her mother preached hadn't included the important facts of life. It was funny really, Fiona thought, that she had run away from home for all the opposite reasons to other teenagers, because her mother never tried to stop her doing anything. Except that the basic reason was the same: Fiona wanted to be free, but freedom for her meant to be able to impose order on her life; to be in control.

A child had had no place in her plans. So she had her daughter adopted. Fiona didn't feel anything. She knew other women would, but she didn't. She handed it over and went to London. There she kept working, learning shorthand and typing at night-school. Then she did business administration and computer studies for a degree at Salthaven College of Arts and Technology. She took opportunities and created openings and used her assets. Now she had a good job in public relations, in line for head of department. Some silly young rapist drowning himself wasn't going to get in the way of that.

They should lie low for a while, though, she told herself. Anyway, it would certainly be some time before she would get Marjorie and Clem to take another degenerate on a punishment trip. Fiona couldn't believe those two didn't seem to get the same kick she did from what they did. They were the ones who really needed the outlet for revenge. For her, the violence was a release. Marjorie and Clem had every reason to feel the same thrill, but they seemed to think they were doing it for the perverts' own good.

Fiona changed her dress. She always dressed as though she expected to be undressed at a moment's notice. Titillation, she knew, was an aspect of female power. This was something else that set her apart from a chronic victim like Clem, who never thought about what she wore, and dressed every day in a track suit or jeans. And, of course, no one ever noticed what Marjorie wore; they simply thanked God she was covered.

When Fiona walked into Frank Borden's office twenty minutes later, she saw him give her the quick once-over, even if he was supposed to be above that sort of thing. Frank Borden was more than a genius in the business world, he was also a moral force. Fiona had often heard the phrase 'moral force' used in connection with Mr Borden but she was not sure what it meant. She took it to mean he didn't play around, even if he was a bachelor and there was no wife to keep him from having fun. She was often told it was a great honour to work for a firm headed by Frank Borden because his name demanded respect everywhere. He gave lectures on business ethics to the Confederation of British Industry and the Institute of Directors. He had actually turned down a knighthood, which she was told showed he would not compromise his religious principles. Mr Borden was a Quaker. She was not clear about what that meant except that he didn't smoke or drink alcohol and wore the same suit and tie to work every day, or at least, a suit and tie that always looked the same.

'No need to be nervous,' Frank Borden said. He knew that this afternoon was important for Fiona. If she did well, she would be confirmed head of the public relations department; if not, someone more experienced would be brought in over her head. 'It's a good security system. It's just the thing for our under-staffed prisons. He's a Home Office adviser on prisons. You've only got to convince him.'

Fiona smiled at him, but she couldn't help saying to herself, you wouldn't say that if I were a man.

Frank Borden walked with her to the foyer to greet their guest. Behind them, the chief engineer tried to chat to the new financial director, Tim Yates, but the young man looked too nervous to respond. As they reached the entrance, Fiona smiled at him. She was looking forward to her big moment.

A car drew up and Fiona was about to step forward. But she couldn't move. The man who got out of the car wasn't the elderly businessman she expected, but a young man who was undoubtedly the most glamorous creature she'd ever seen.

She wouldn't have been able to define exactly what she meant, or what she intended to do about it. She simply recognized the young man as exactly the kind of person she needed to get her what she wanted. She had no doubt about it.

She heard Frank Borden make an irritated click of the tongue. 'Oh, no, not that idiot son! He's sent the damned monkey,' he said in her ear. She had never heard Frank swear before. Then he stepped forward to greet his unwelcome guest.

The young man shook Frank Borden's hand. 'My father sends his apologies, Frank, but he's been struck down with this bug that's going round. It was too late to cancel, so he asked me to step in.'

Frank Borden turned to her. 'Bruce, this is Fiona Farr.'

Fiona looked into deep dark-blue eyes. Through a haze she heard Frank Borden explaining that Bruce Wheeler was working as his father's right-hand man running the Wheeler empire. Frank didn't sound convinced that his old friend Tom was doing the right thing, but there was no doubt that the son was being groomed to take over. Fiona sensed his disappointment.

Bruce Wheeler shook her hand, and said her name as though she was something

43

delicious to eat. Fiona had always recognized opportunity when she saw it. All her instincts for self-interest told her to make an impression on Bruce Wheeler. She had a job to do. She was good at it. She answered Bruce Wheeler's questions and explained the new security system so that even the blasé technical journalists and local reporters were interested.

It was exciting. Bruce Wheeler smiled at her, not only smiled but also looked into her eyes as though she were the only person in the room. It set her apart from the rest of the people there. It's good fun standing beside him, she thought, like a foretaste of things to come. For once in my life, she told herself, here's a truly big fish.

She tried to remember what she had read about him in gossip magazines. She thought he'd featured often in articles headlined Britain's Most Eligible Men. But after that there was never anything much to read about except his string of girlfriends and his appearances at society parties. He was rich and young and glamorous, and that seemed to be about it. Fiona hadn't been particularly interested. He was yet another important father's playboy son. What Fiona hadn't realized until now was that the playboy was the designated crown prince to the Wheeler industrial and media empire.

There was only one incident which threatened to sour her day. When her presentation was over, she took a brief break in a cubicle in the Ladies room to gather her thoughts. A group of journalists came in and started chatting in front of the mirror. Fiona opened the cubicle door slightly to watch them.

'Our Brucie's on form today,' one said. She had a strong South London accent.

'The little local number doesn't know what's hit her,' another said. 'Talk about willing to the slaughter.'

'Poor kid, perhaps someone should warn her,' said the South Londoner.

'Are you kidding? That little man-trap? I think Brucie's bitten off more than he can chew there,' said an older woman putting vivid lipstick on her thin lips. 'I wouldn't mind seeing her get a slapping myself.'

'It's no joke. He put one of those would-be models who hang around the Fitness Centre in hospital. Beat her up quite badly, the story goes,' a new voice offered. She was a reporter from the local paper, glad to have something to contribute to the gossip of London journalists. She added, 'Of course it was hushed up. It didn't get into the paper.'

The London women weren't interested in

neighbourhood gossip and speculation. They ignored the local reporter. Soon they were gone. Fiona was left smarting at being called 'the little local number'. Patronizing bitches, she thought. Then she dismissed them from her mind. Bruce Wheeler would be waiting for her to take him into lunch. They're just jealous, she told herself. Ugly cows, all of them, as if Bruce Wheeler would give one of them a second glance.

Fiona fiddled with the unbuttoned buttons at her cleavage. She didn't even notice, as she led Bruce Wheeler into the chief engineer's office for drinks before lunch, that the television in the room had not been turned off. She didn't hear a sombre-faced newsreader announce that the body of a young man had been found washed up on the shore near Salthaven.

5

Clem had lost the knack of passing time doing nothing. Without some sort of physical activity on which to concentrate, she couldn't stop herself thinking. She didn't want to think; not about Naylor, not about what she was going to do with her life; not about Martin Bakewell: most of all, not about her mother and father. At this moment, her mother would be in the kitchen creating work for herself, and her dad would be sitting in his armchair by the dead fire reading the paper and grumbling under his breath about the state of the world. And they would both, she knew, be thinking of her. Clem hadn't allowed herself to wonder why she had cut herself off from them since she was raped. She meant to write. She'd started letters trying to explain, but so far she hadn't come up with an explanation. It's cruel, she thought, I'm being cruel. I know what it must be doing to them. I've only got to look at Marjorie to know that. But I can't, not yet. I know they love me, but I can't.

'I've got to get out of here,' she said, and her own voice startled her in the silence.

She went out on her mountain bike, put her head down, and peddled furiously up hills and across rough tracks on the Common, hoping to blot out everything but the wind and the sky and the straining of muscle. She drove forward harder and harder as the road began to climb steeply out of the town. She heard the rasp of her own breathing. Her legs began to ache and her knuckles were white on the handlebars. At the summit, the road flattened out. It was too easy. She turned the bike and fled back down the hill on the public road. She could hardly see where she was going. The camber of the road steered her. She sped across the main road at the lights at the bottom of the hill. If I don't get hit, she told herself, the young man is alive. Then, unscathed, she set out along the beach road towards the harbour.

A board outside a newsagent's had the latest local news printed in tall spindly black letters. Clem swerved. A passing motorist swore at her. She had to put her foot on the kerb to stop. Leaning forward over the handlebars she read the headline in the evening paper about a body washed up naked on the beach.

They'd done it, then. They'd killed him. She thought of the young man naked in the cold dark sea, tiring, unable to keep afloat, gasping as the foul salt black water closed over his head.

She cycled on slowly. It had started to rain. Lorries hissed past her, drenching her in the spray from their wheels. In the Dock Road, by the steamed-up window of Bert's Café, she was held up in a tailback of traffic. It was a grey dismal afternoon cheered only by the lights in the café windows.

Then the door of Bert's opened and a man came out. No, Clem thought, it can't be. It must be someone like him. The man was coming towards her across the road between the stationary vehicles. He looked directly at her but he didn't recognize her. It was Terry Naylor; she could swear it was. But Naylor had moved away from Salthaven. Naylor's mother, whose name was not Naylor but something else, had started a campaign to have men accused of rape called 'Mr X' in court so that the innocent could be protected. In her letters to the local newspaper, Naylor's mother claimed her son had been driven out of town even though he had been found innocent in court. It wasn't Naylor.

Clem watched the man dart out of the way of a bus. Now she was not sure. He no longer looked to her exactly like Naylor. But she had been sure only a moment before, as sure as she had been when she identified him as her attacker in court. It's guilt, she told herself. I feel guilty about the other one drowning in that cold dark water, and I'm seeing things.

6

But it was Naylor. When he came back to Salthaven, Terry Naylor went to live with his mother. She was over-protective, babying him every chance she got. He hated that, and the poky little house she'd been forced to find because there wasn't much demand for her interior designing skills after his court case. She called it a 'bijou country cottage', but he thought it was a peasant's hovel. He blamed her for that. It wouldn't have happened if she hadn't made such a fuss about the way her poor son had been treated, being accused and pilloried so that his life was ruined although he was innocent. That hadn't done her any good at all; or him either. He would have moved out but he didn't have enough money to support himself in anything like the style he thought he should expect. His mother complained about him having such a lowly, lonely job. She said she'd spent money sending him to a private boarding-school and he should be able to do better than nightwatchman in a furniture factory. She should have realized that he preferred to work alone at night after what happened when his life had been ruined by that tart who'd tried to resist him and pulled off his balaclava and got a good look at him. She'd been the first to fight back. The others had been too terrified to move.

Naylor often talked to himself as if the gentlemen of the jury might be listening. He'd only given those girls a good seeing too, and it wasn't as if they were innocents; they were university students and nurses at Salthaven Hospital, and even, once, a young constable in the police section house. She hadn't struggled, just begged him to stop. And the more she begged, he said to himself, with no fear of eavesdroppers, the harder he'd slammed it into her. He began to feel quite cheerful, thinking about it. Most women would love to get their hands on a man like me, he thought, they'd pay money for it. And secretly, she must have loved it. It stood to reason. If they do it for fun, which that bitch who'd gone for him had probably done plenty, then they'd got to be having a good time getting it even when they were crying out they couldn't take it any more. It was their nature. There must be something wrong with English society that made them not dare to admit the fun they were having when it gets slammed into them like that by a real man. A real man like himself. That's what he was. There was no doubt about that. Naylor started to feel good.

Working nights, he usually slept most of the day, but today his mother wouldn't let him alone so he left the house at noon. He'd thought of going down to the martial arts centre for a training session, but for once he didn't feel like it. Usually he spent at least two hours each day training. He took his kick-boxing seriously, and it was physically demanding. He wasn't like one of those wankers who pumped iron at the poncy Fitness Centre downtown where some of his colleagues on the day shift did a few circuits and thought they'd really worked out.

He found himself at the factory. He went into the cubby hole that was his office. He watched the workers through the grille. There was a good deal of laughing and joking. He thought, what do they think they've got to be so cheery about? He felt contempt for their cheerfulness. He flexed the muscles of his shoulders under the security guard's uniform. He had a powerful body. The workers were puny in comparison; and many of them were old, showing signs of decay. They were also stupid, they laughed and joked among themselves as though there was nothing wrong with them, as though they were not feeble and decaying. He looked at them, at how ugly they were, and he swelled with pride thinking of his own bodily perfection.

But the sight of them depressed him. With time to kill, he went out to Bert's Café in the Dock Road. The air inside Bert's smelled of stale cigarette smoke and fried onions. The place was full of men. Naylor never saw a woman there, except for Bert's fat Italian wife and his three plump daughters. The daughters screamed Italian-style abuse in English at the customers as they served them. The girls had never been to Italy. It was their joke. The youngest daughter, Mary, was not bad-looking. Naylor thought she fancied him although she never said anything. She must know that he would never look at a girl like her.

He liked to sit at a small table by the window. If someone got there before him, he would sit at another table close by glowering at the intruder until the man began to squirm with discomfort and eat quickly and leave.

But this afternoon his seat was free and Mary, the looker, was working. A group of lorry drivers, men too bulky for the cramped plastic table and chairs, were eating breakfast. They never ate anything else. They were making far too much noise and on top of that, the radio was blaring from the shelf above the hotplate. Naylor never played the radio. The nightwatchman before him at the furniture factory had left one behind, but Naylor never used it. He liked silence. He could think. He liked thought. He did a lot of thinking. At work he also liked listening to his own metal-tipped footsteps echoing powerfully through the rafters of the gloomy building. There was menace in that sound. He liked thinking about menace.

The music stopped. A man started to read the news. The lorry drivers at the crowded table fell silent. They wanted to hear reports of roadworks and heavy traffic.

A moment later, Naylor exclaimed, 'What did he say? What did that bloke just say?'

'What you complaining about now?' Mary said, passing by his table with her arms full of dirty dishes.

'What was that news?' Naylor asked.

One of the drivers folded his newspaper and pushed it across the table to Naylor.

'No, not that,' Naylor said. 'On the radio. They said about a body.'

The driver said, 'They found a body washed up on a beach with mystery marks on his back.'

'Not marks,' another driver said. 'He said weals.'

'Weals are marks,' the first driver said.

Naylor said, 'They didn't say he'd been

whipped, did they?'

'Yeah,' the driver said, 'weals like from a whip.'

Naylor could feel goose pimples on the back of his neck in spite of the steamy heat in the café. His mouth was dry. Those weals on the corpse's back might keep the police guessing, but not Naylor. He knew what they meant.

He had marks on his own back.

It's them, Naylor thought. They've gone too far this time, they've really done it now. They're murderers.

He sat on over an empty plate, waiting for a longer report on the radio. The lorry drivers left after the weather forecast and the local road reports, but he sat on. Mary brought him another mug of tea without being asked. Clearly she expected him to ask her to sit down with him while business was quiet. But he ignored her and she went away, tossing her head.

When the detailed report came on, he heard a girl reporter on the spot tell how the police thought the man had jumped off the Mullein Head rocks into the sea and been dragged round into the estuary by the tide. Or he might have been carried down by the current from further up-river.

But Naylor knew better than that. He knew

the dead man had been out on the same boat he had. He knew about the women. He knew what those man-hating cats did. They'd trapped him too. They'd fooled him that night after he was released from the remand centre.

He'd been in a pub. There'd been this woman there. A real looker with a nice arse; a blonde, small, she'd come snaking up to him, looking sexy in dark glasses. She'd been wearing tight white shorts that almost cut her in half. He'd suspected nothing.

She'd taken him out to a boat on a temporary mooring on Falloden Creek. She told him to call her Tizzy, short for some long Greek name — Tisiphone. She wasn't Greek. He could tell that. She spoke with a plummy English accent.

She took him out in a rubber dingy through huddles of mooring lights and dark stretches of water where he could not see her face, only the blonde hair, silver-plated in the moonlight.

She brought the dinghy alongside the shadowy hull of a yacht, about a thirty-footer, with a ladder up the side. He went up the ladder after her, watching that beautiful arse moving in the little shorts.

There were two other women on board, wearing Mickey and Minnie Mouse masks.

They had Greek names, too. They said the names, and then told him to call them Meg and Ali. He'd got it then; they were all posh bints on the pull giving phoney names so he wouldn't know who they really were. Maybe they were celebrities. He'd heard of celebrities and posh bints going out to bars and discos dressed up as ordinary people. If they were on the pull, he could see they wouldn't want to be recognized. He smiled at them, a smile that showed he understood. Then they'd gone for him.

They were perverts. The two in masks held him down while the little blonde flogged him till he couldn't even scream with pain. Then they'd told him they were punishing him because he'd escaped justice for what he'd done to that stupid university student who'd tried to put the finger on him.

Afterwards they tied his hands and blindfolded him. Then they took him in the dinghy and put him off in a cove up the coast. They just left him like that on the beach, in such pain. He could see nothing with the blindfold, naked in the cold with his hands tied behind his back. The bitches had dropped his good clothes on the wet sand. There was no sign of the yacht. He'd sworn then that he would make them pay. He'd told himself he'd kill the lot of them if he found them, leaving that little blonde till last. But he couldn't imagine who they were.

He'd told his mother he'd been beaten up by thugs in the street. She'd wanted him to go to the police, or to hospital, but he persuaded her that it was best to lie low with animals like that. He thought they might come after him if he grassed on them, and he wasn't ready for them yet. He wouldn't let his mother touch him, but he'd gone to bed for two days.

Then he'd gone looking for the blonde and her friends in the masks, searching the boats in the marina and on the Falloden Creek moorings until he was feeling crazy about the injustice of it all. They weren't there. He decided they must be out-of-towners who'd hunted him down and then made off to wherever they came from. At last he left town and went away from Salthaven altogether. But he still vowed revenge on those women. He thought about it. He had dreams about it. But away from home he couldn't find work that suited him. He would rather live off his mother than do something he didn't like. He came back to Salthaven and moved in with her in her poky cottage.

Naylor never let his mother see the marks on his back. Once he was back in Salthaven, no one saw his scars. He kept them covered all the time. He always wore a T-shirt when he was training and never took a shower at the National Martial Arts Centre in River Street. Other people might think it odd that he didn't wash but no one dared to say.

And all that time he didn't forget the three bitches. How could he?

Now here was this story on the radio and he knew that they were in Salthaven again.

Mary came over to clear his table. 'You all right?' she asked. 'You look cold. You were shivering like you're coming down with something.'

'I'm all right,' he said.

He went out. He was crossing to the bus stop when a bicycle came at him out of the rain. A girl with very short hair sped by but not before he saw her look at him with wide eyes. It was the same way Mary looked at him. The girl on the bicycle had noticed him and he must have looked like the answer to her prayers. He smiled. Naylor felt good again.

He took a bus to the marina. It had once been a village fishing harbour but it had been overrun by the sprawling suburbs. Only a few metres remained of the old harbour wall. They had put some boutiques and restaurants and bars round the old marine engineering works, but business hadn't been good. It was empty and disused now. He liked it that way. He liked seeing the empty shop fronts boarded up and the filth blowing around in the whining wind.

The boats in the marina bobbed and dipped against the pontoons. Most of them were still laid up as if it were winter. Around them there was the usual swirl of sea birds. When he walked out on to the slatted wooden platform the jangling and clanking of the wind in the rigging of the boats disturbed him. He hated the wind.

He found the watchman's hut. It was locked. Across the road from the marina entrance was a pub. He thought the watchman would be there at this time of day.

A frumpy young woman appeared from somewhere in the back. Naylor could hear a baby crying. He ordered a pint. She kept looking over her shoulder to where the baby was crying as she waited for the beer to settle.

Naylor said, 'You know the nightwatchman from the marina?'

'You mean Ted?'

'I suppose I do if he's the nightwatchman.' He spoke in his most public school accent to assert his superiority, a man like him coming into a place like this.

'That's Ted. Over there.' She turned her

head and nodded to an old drunk sitting in the corner.

'One for him,' Naylor said. She pulled a second pint.

Naylor took the pints across to the corner table. The old man looked up trying to see if he recognized Naylor.

'Bought you a drink,' Naylor said.

Ted said nothing. Naylor sat down.

It was heavy going. The old man was drunk and Naylor had had little practice in talking to people.

Then a look of bleary cunning crossed Ted's face. 'You from the company?' he said. 'Who sent you here?'

'No, no,' Naylor said, 'I'm on your side. I'm not from the company. I'm a watchman too. I do nights.'

'At night I think,' Ted said, 'that's what I do at night.'

Naylor said, 'I've a friend likes to sail out at night. She's got a thirty-footer. You know her? She's small and blonde, a looker, lots of money.'

'There's a woman on one of them boats like that but she's not a blonde. Dark as a crow. What do you want to know for?'

'I met her once. But the one I met was a blonde.'

'The one I know, she's no blonde.'

'It was a long time ago I knew her,' Naylor said. 'She used to sail at nights then. She probably stays home nights now.'

'She doesn't stay home if it's the one I mean. Her boat's on berth thirty-six,' the old man said as if he was angry. 'That's another thing you don't know. She went out two nights ago.' He sounded pleased, knowing something Naylor didn't know.

'You saw her go out?'

'I saw her come back,' he said. 'Two o'clock in the morning. I was on my way out to take a piss, and I heard the church clock. I may not have seen her go, but I saw her come back. Her and those two friends of hers, one old enough to be her mother, and one who could be a boy or a girl, by the looks of her, looks more like a lad, one of those Afrodites in the Sunday paper.'

'Hermaphrodites,' Naylor corrected him automatically. Ted slumped in his chair. He would say no more.

Naylor went out and walked back to the marina. There was still no one around. Sea birds gathered about the rubbish bins screeching. Gulls, perched on the deckrails of the boats tied to the pontoon, lurched slowly into the air as he made his way across the slatted platform. He did not like the feeling of the planks moving. He steadied himself

63

against the hulls of the boats.

He found berth thirty-six on the furthest pontoon from the shore. There was a boat tied up there. It was a thirty footer, an old Arpège, painted dark blue. The hatch cover was padlocked. Naylor read the name painted in white across her dark blue stern. He spelled out the word, *Eumenides*, and then Salthaven. This was her home port. The name *Eumenides* meant nothing to him. He'd never done Latin and Greek at school. He wasn't in the classics stream. He wasn't what they called university material. He tried to pronounce the word phonetically; a stupid name; like Tisiphone and Alecto and Megaera.

Naylor felt proud of himself. He felt like a detective who'd done a good job with a clue all the others had overlooked but not him.

7

It was a perfect evening for wandering round a summer garden but Marjorie had not made up her mind to go. The invitation card was propped against the beaded evening-bag on the kitchen counter: Dr and Mrs Oliver Tate requested the pleasure of her company at the house-warming of their new home.

Janet Tate had never requested the pleasure of Marjorie Warren's company, not ever. It had always been Ben she'd wanted, and because Oliver Tate was influential and very wealthy, Ben had insisted that the two Warrens spent a lot of time at Janet Tate's parties in the old days.

Marjorie thought Janet must have sent her the new invitation by mistake. She must have forgotten that Nathalie was now the Mrs Warren who counted. But there was a note scrawled on the back of the card: 'Please come, Tom Wheeler will be here, and he was asking about Tessa the other day. Perhaps he wants to reopen the case?'

Marjorie's first reaction was to rip the card to shreds. How could Janet Tate write a note like that, as though someone had asked her for a recipe or something.

Then she thought, perhaps Tom Wheeler really could help. Perhaps he's the one man alive who might stir things up. He'd made a fuss before, when the police first lost interest. If the case were reopened, there might be some scrap of information that'd been overlooked. If only I knew if she was dead or alive, I think I could bear it, Marjorie said to herself, it's the not knowing I can't stand.

Marjorie had always disliked parties, particularly parties on warm evenings in summer gardens, where wasps threatened every sip of a drink, and midges always seemed to plague her more than anyone else.

But Tom Wheeler would be there. She admired him. On television, in colour, he appeared perhaps rather too bronzed and flashy, with all that white hair and his rather studied, gleaming, smile. She preferred him in newspapers where she perceived an added gloss of intelligence and subtlety in the shadows and angles of black and white photography. She thought he would make a good Prime Minister. As the power behind the throne, though, he didn't have to go through the sordid process of getting elected. Marjorie couldn't see Tom Wheeler kissing babies or sitting toddlers on his knee. If they weren't politicians, Marjorie thought, they'd be accused of child abuse. Tom Wheeler had power without that. His media interests alone were global now.

'Yes,' she said to Queenie, the cat, who was snaking round her ankles looking to be fed, 'I'll never forgive myself if he could really help me.'

Oddly, the death of the young man who'd jumped off the stern of Fiona's boat had forced her to face the fact that she must push her way back among normal people some day soon or accept she wasn't quite sane. She would never get an easier first step than this. In a garden, if no one spoke to her, she could pretend an interest in the plants. And she had a real purpose in going.

So she left the house and drove the battered old Deux Chevaux to the wealthy suburb where the Tates had built themselves their new house. She told herself she could always give it the once over and, if Tom Wheeler didn't turn up, she'd turn round and go home.

Outside the gates she parked the car and sat watching people going into the party. They were all in groups or couples. Marjorie couldn't see anyone else on their own. She put the car key back in the ignition. Why put herself through it? She didn't have to.

Then someone tapped on the car window.

'Marjorie, it's wonderful to see you. Let me help.' Oliver Tate opened the car door and held out his hand to help her out. There was no escape now.

Marjorie walked up the sweeping front steps to Janet Tate. 'Is Tom Wheeler here yet?' she asked. It was only when she saw the look of shock on Janet's face that she realized how rude she sounded. 'It's a beautiful house,' she said. She had to say something.

'We like it,' Janet Tate said and managed to look as if she had run the place up with her own hands. She caught the arm of a man. He was an elderly man with white whiskers. 'Here,' Janet Tate said, 'you two know each other, don't you? You take my very good friend Marjorie Warren out into the garden and get her a drink. The bar's in the conservatory.'

The elderly man looked at Marjorie without interest.

'Of course,' he said. 'Delighted.'

He walked ahead of her through double doors into the terraced garden.

She needed a drink. Her hands were trembling. There were waiters. She could see their white coats and trays but they were always somewhere else.

The white-haired man didn't wait to ask what she would like before moving away through the crowd towards the bar in the conservatory. 'Well, that's the last I'll see of him,' she said.

'I beg your pardon?' a man said.

Marjorie was horrified to find she had spoken aloud. 'I'm sorry,' she said. She did not raise her eyes. 'Excuse me.'

'Hey, wait a minute,' the man said. 'Don't I know you?'

Marjorie looked up. It was Tom Wheeler.

'My daughter,' she said, 'when she went missing? Tessa Warren. You were kind . . . '

He nodded. 'It must have been terrible for you. Our children have such terrible power to hurt us, don't they? How is she now, your, er, Teresa? No more trouble, I hope?'

It was as though he had knifed her. She felt the blood draining from her face. She was sure she was going to faint.

'No,' she managed to say, 'no trouble at all. She's still missing. And, Mr Wheeler, our children may have terrible power to hurt us, but it's as nothing to the damage stupid, insensitive strangers can do without even trying.'

Marjorie had to take the smug look of concern off his face. She slapped him, hard.

She saw his stunned expression as she pushed past him, stumbling towards the front door.

There was a small group of people in the hall. She couldn't face them, she couldn't let anyone see her in this state.

Then she was stopped in her tracks, astounded to see Fiona standing in the middle of this sociable group, all smiles. The girl said something to Janet Tate's husband that made him laugh.

She heard Fiona call her name. 'Leave me alone,' Marjorie heard herself snarl. She pushed Fiona aside as she barged through the group in the hallway as she ran to the front door.

'What's got into her?' someone asked.

Fiona's laughter mocked her. 'A menopausal madwoman,' she said.

8

Fiona hadn't been invited to the garden party. Frank Borden had rung her at home two days after Bruce Wheeler's visit to the office and told her he wanted her there. 'As my escort', he'd said. Fiona saw the invitation to mean that the promotion to Head of the Public Relations Department was as good as hers. She agreed to pick him up and drive him there.

'But do me a favour,' Fiona said, 'if you introduce me to anyone, make it clear I'm not your secretary. It's really humiliating when people think a woman with someone important is his secretary.'

Frank Borden laughed.

'I'm not joking,' Fiona said. 'You don't know what it's like.'

'Good heavens, what's wrong with being a secretary?' Frank Borden said.

'There speaks someone who has never been taken for one.' She tried to make a joke of it, but she sounded firm. This was something that mattered a lot to her.

'No one's going to think you're my secretary,' Frank said. 'Anyway, I want you to

71

carry on the good work you did with Bruce Wheeler.'

And he was the first person she saw there. Fiona was excited. She was determined to impress Bruce Wheeler. She was well aware that it wouldn't be difficult to have an affair with him, but that wasn't enough. It seemed to Fiona that being at an important party with Frank Borden was the perfect first step to making Bruce Wheeler see her as someone to be taken seriously.

And then that idiot Marjorie had spoiled everything by causing a hysterical scene. After that, the party turned into a nightmare.

Apart from anything else, Fiona now had to worry about what else Marjorie might do. The woman was plainly out of control. At the party Fiona had been able to deny any connection with her. She had been careful to make it clear she hadn't seen her for ages, though she'd once known her daughter, the girl who disappeared and had never been seen again.

But if the police had been called, as they might well have been, Marjorie might have claimed Fiona as a character witness. The last thing Fiona wanted was the police asking questions. She'd kept it very quiet, even from Clem and Marjorie, but she had a police record. When she was younger, she'd been a bit fiery. She'd kicked in the dashboard of a car. There'd been a few disruptive scenes in restaurants, and criminal damage to a boyfriend's flat. Fiona liked breaking glass. She liked the sound of it. The boyfriend, claiming to be afraid for his life, called the police, and then there was resisting arrest. Fiona didn't want to be dragged into Marjorie's shenanigans.

Fiona also blamed Marjorie for what happened with Bruce Wheeler later. It was that which had turned the party into a nightmare.

Fiona, a firm advocate of turning disaster to her own advantage where possible, had decided to use Marjorie's verbal attack on herself, practically spitting at her and pushing her out of her way, as a reason for approaching Bruce Wheeler to ask if his father, Marjorie's other victim, was all right.

'I was coming to find *you*,' Bruce told her. 'Are you OK?'

'Oh, yes, I'm fine. It was just so unexpected.'

'What can have got into the woman? My father says he was talking to her as friendly as anything and she suddenly lashed out at him. She shouldn't be allowed out.'

'It's probably her age,' Fiona said.

'Well, as long as you're all right,' he said,

looking deep into her eyes. 'Ever since I first saw you, I've been meaning to ring you and ask you for a little private tuition. I'm sure you could teach me a tremendous lot if you would.'

The party was in full swing around them. He had almost to whisper in her ear or she wouldn't have been able to make out what he was saying.

Fiona closed her eyes for a moment, then opened them very wide, swayed, and put her hand on his sleeve. 'I'm sorry,' she said faintly, 'I think it's the shock. I've got to get some air.'

At once Bruce Wheeler led her out of the crowded room through the open french windows into the shadows of the twilit garden.

'Better?' he asked. He kept his arm firmly round her shoulders, pressing her against him as he took her to a stone bench screened by a pergola of full-blown white roses.

She sat there and he sat beside her, still supporting her. She could feel his heart thumping against her temple.

'Well?' she said, moving closer to him.

'What?'

She laughed. 'What's making you so coy all of a sudden? What do you think we're doing out here, for God's sake?'

The light on the terrace was too dim for her to see his expression.

'Are you feeling better?' he asked.

There was sudden silence as someone closed the french windows on the noise of the party and drew the curtains. The terrace was in darkness.

Fiona reached up and drew his head down. For a moment his lips were hard against hers; then she opened her mouth. She wanted him. She wanted him to make love to her right there on the cold stone bench. She didn't care if anyone came out onto the terrace and saw them.

'No!' He broke away from her. He pushed her down so that she sprawled half-naked on the stone bench.

'What are you doing?' she said. 'I want you, it's all right.'

'Are you mad?' he said. There was something about his tone of voice that alarmed her. There was fear in it, but also disgust and, worse even than that, contempt.

When it came to sex, Fiona was used to being in control with men. She thought, he's playing hard to get.

'Come on, Bruce, no one can see. It's too dark.'

What he said then she couldn't believe.

'Stop it, you little tramp,' he said.

'Everyone who is anyone in this area is in that room. My *father* is there, for God's sake. What makes you think I'd risk being caught giving Frank Borden's hick little secretary a seeing to in a respectable place like this?'

'What did you say?' she said. 'What did you fucking say?'

But he'd left her. She saw him framed in the light of the french windows as he opened them. He smoothed his hair with both hands, then stepped over the ledge into the still crowded party. He closed the glass doors firmly behind him.

Fiona wanted to kill Bruce Wheeler, *really* kill him. Secretary! He'd called her Frank Borden's hick secretary. He'd turned her down because he couldn't face his up-market friends seeing him with her.

Her first thought was to walk into the party, go up to Bruce Wheeler and hit him just like Marjorie had hit his father. But that was no good. *She'd* be the laughing stock, not him.

Her mind was crawling with all the things she might have said and done to him if she could replay the scene now.

'You're going to pay for this,' she said aloud. 'I'll get even. You're going to wish you were dead by the time I've finished with you.'

Without realizing what she was doing, she

began to tear the shadowy white blooms of the roses, scattering the petals on the terrace. Then she walked around the outside of the house to the drive where she had parked her car. Frank Borden could get a taxi home.

Fiona, facing the empty evening, didn't want to be alone. She tried to think of someone she could ring on her mobile phone. Then she thought of Tim Yates, the company's new finance director. He had only joined the firm that week, and his family was still in Birmingham. He was staying at the Excelsior Hotel while looking for a house to buy once the Birmingham home was sold, which looked like taking a long while to do.

Fiona found him at the Excelsior. 'I can't bear to think of you stuck there on your own,' she said. 'It's miserable being in hotels, isn't it?'

Half an hour later she walked into his room. He's not bad-looking, she thought, but he's such a plump little married man, already half bald from the responsibilities of being a grown-up businessman, husband and father. She knew about those responsibilities, she could see the photos on the bedside table, wife and two kids. The wife looked disapproving as though the photographer had just said something wrong.

He was hard going. At one point during the

evening Fiona nearly decided to go home alone. He wasn't much fun. He wasn't even really attractive. But it was easier to go through with it. They were in his room.

'Not here,' she said, 'not now. I don't want to anymore, not here.'

'What's the matter?'

'We shouldn't do it here,' she said. 'Someone might say something to your wife.' She disentangled herself and stood up. 'We'll go to the boat. You'll like the boat. No one will know. It won't be like desecrating the matrimonial hotel bedroom.'

'You know,' he said, 'I've never met a girl like you before.'

'No,' she said, 'I don't suppose you have.'

9

Hobbs now knew the identity of the body on the mudflats. He was Martin Bakewell, an alleged rapist. He was twenty-one and a university graduate. He had picked up a thirteen-year-old schoolgirl, Teresa Dixon, and he had raped her. He'd buggered her and then beat her up. That's what she'd said, anyway. Then she'd killed herself. By the time she told her story there was no medical evidence of the attack. It didn't help that she'd been under the local school psychologist for nearly two years because of her anti-social behaviour. Bakewell got the benefit of the doubt.

But Hobbs didn't believe the weals on Martin Bakewell's body were self-inflicted or sado-masochistic sex play that had gone wrong. Hobbs had an idea that Bakewell had been beaten in revenge for the rape, then dumped into the sea to drown. That was murder. Bakewell might be a nasty piece of work but the law didn't allow people to flog nasty pieces of work and then throw them into the sea. Maybe it should, but it didn't.

When Hobbs got to the station Detective

Sergeant Howard was waiting for him.

'We've got an ID on the drowning,' Sergeant Howard said.

'I know,' Hobbs said. 'Martin Bakewell.'

Sergeant Howard looked surprised that Hobbs knew.

Hobbs said, 'I was going through the files. I ran into Bakewell's picture. I recognized him.'

Sergeant Howard was no longer surprised. This was what he expected from Hobbs. Hobbs was keen. He stayed on in the office after his shift was over, like a schoolboy swat.

'I remember the case,' Sergeant Howard said. 'There was a lot of fuss at the time. Probation for sex with a minor. Teresa Dixon's family were pissed off. They thought they were being shafted, which, of course, they were, but they should have been used to it by then. They're all villains. The father and all the brothers. The mother was on the game. She came from a family of villains, too.'

Hobbs said, 'So it could have been them?'

'A vendetta?' Sergeant Howard spoke the word with relish. It amused him to imagine the Dixons, cowboy plumbers and small-time criminals, turning into Sicilians.

'Well?' Hobbs asked. 'Do you think they did it?'

Sergeant Howard made a face as he considered. 'I don't know I'd blame them,' he said. 'That's a right little nancy trick that, buggering a young girl.'

'I'd blame them,' Hobbs said. 'I would. We can't have people taking the law into their own hands.'

'You're too young,' Sergeant Howard said. 'You don't know what a father feels about his daughter. If it was my daughter I'd kill the bastard, or I'd have him killed. I could do that, you know, I could have a man like that put down and no one would be the wiser.' He smiled thinking of his secret powers. But he didn't have a daughter to protect, only sons.

Hobbs said, 'We can't have that. We couldn't do our job properly if everyone did that.'

'Not many people say we do our job properly anyway,' Sergeant Howard said. 'That's why they take the law into their own hands.' He sounded sad and resigned now, no longer full of Sicilian vengeance. 'Well, anyway,' he said, 'there's no evidence connecting the Dixons with it, and they're not the type to drown a bloke peacefully. The Dixons would go in for something a bit uglier than that, like impaling him on a stake, or cutting his cock off. We've got to accept the obvious. Young Bakewell was drunk, and he fell off a rock into the sea. Or he was a nice sensitive young man who couldn't live with the horrible thing he'd done so he gave himself a token lash with a whip and then went for a final swim.'

'The whip marks weren't token.'

'Well, he was a faggot who whipped himself.' Sergeant Howard was pleased with himself. He started talking as if he were describing a wonderful meal he'd had in a restaurant. 'He buggered the girl, didn't he? That's a faggot trick. Whipping yourself is faggot stuff. So's getting a chum to whip you.'

'It's worth making a few inquiries, isn't it?'

'Look, son, at the moment we've more work on than we can handle. I got two off sick. Another one's on fucking paternity leave and one off with period pains. Ask yourself, does it really matter? The nasty little twat's dead and gone. He was a victim of tragic circumstance. Or the bugger got sensible and topped himself. He won't be sorely missed.'

Hobbs shook his head. He couldn't agree. 'Think what it would mean if we worked on the basis you're talking about. The system would break down.'

'The system? You think the system hasn't already broken down? Anyway, we can't help the way we feel.'

'Even the victim wouldn't want us to feel like you do,' Hobbs said. As he said it, he thought this was probably not true, but he still hoped that it was.

'Who gives a fuck what the victim thinks?' Sergeant Howard said. 'Being a rape victim doesn't give her some special extra rights. She's just another case history.'

Sergeant Howard smiled. He liked giving worldly wisdom to Hobbs, who was immature in many ways. Hobbs had not come to grips with the evil that infested the world. But Hobbs was odd. He had a girlfriend but she was the wrong sort of girl for him to have. She was a married woman, and not young. Fellows like Hobbs shouldn't be tied down to some older married woman with complications. He should be playing the field at his age. There were plenty about who were begging for it. It was surprising that Hobbs should be knocking about with an older married woman and still be a knight in shining armour to the opposite sex. Hobbs was given to chivalrous acts. Already he had almost got himself dismissed from the Force. He'd had a go at some yobs menacing a couple of professional tarts, real genuine whores, outside a pub at closing time. In those circles, Sergeant Howard reckoned, what the yobs were doing was no more than foreplay, but Hobbs had weighed in and got himself brought in for brawling. When the whores found out he was a copper they laughed themselves silly. They'd never heard of such a thing.

'You can laugh,' Hobbs said, though Sergeant Howard was not laughing. 'I believe in the system. It's all we've got. I couldn't do this job if I didn't believe in it.'

'Couldn't do your job? Don't be soft. You do your job for the pay cheque and the pension. Who are you trying to kid?'

Hobbs picked up the notes on his desk. 'There's no harm in asking a few questions about what Teresa Dixon's father was doing on the night in question.'

Sergeant Howard looked smug. 'It's already done,' he said. 'If you'd been in earlier, you'd know. He couldn't have done it. He's on remand. He's been in custody for six months.'

'What about the Dixon brothers?'

'What about the brothers?'

'Where were they?'

'One's dead. One's in hospital. The other one's in Manchester.'

'Maybe he came down from Manchester,' Hobbs said.

'He's in Strangeways in Manchester.'

Sergeant Howard had checked the Dixons out. He wouldn't have minded fitting them up for the Bakewell death, even if he really thought it was suicide.

'I still think we should look a bit deeper,' Hobbs said.

All sorts of people were taking the law into their own hands. They saw themselves as concerned citizens who didn't think punishments fitted the crimes around them. Or, Hobbs thought, they were carried away by the thought of secret power, like Howard was when he said he could have a man done in and no one would be the wiser. Hobbs thought there must be many out there in the streets longing for that secret power, especially those who thought themselves hard done by in life. Then Hobbs thought, I think of them as men but it's just as likely to be women who feel hard done by and long for secret power. It's women who use poison and watch it quietly take effect. They would love secret power more than a man, who would want to show his power off.

Hobbs was not going to drop the Martin Bakewell case. Sergeant Howard had been too long at the job. He was too cynical. He was a bitter and disappointed man who had given up hopes of promotion. If Sergeant Howard had been a good detective, Hobbs told himself, he'd have done better than sergeant at his age.

When Hobbs had cleared his desk, he thought he should ring Annie. He would have to placate her about not going to see her last night. He felt guilty about Annie because she was in a difficult position. But, with her husband away on the oil rigs in the Middle East, she was hardly married at all. When the husband came home once a year, Annie said he knocked her about. She said she wanted to start having some fun. She said, 'I'm still young. I want to go out and have some fun.' When he made love to her she went wild but he couldn't help feeling that he was buying her. She laughed at him. 'I like thinking of us being together and him not knowing,' she said, 'it makes me feel good after what he's made me suffer.' Besides, she said it was all right because Hobbs loved her and she loved him.

On the phone she said, 'What happened last night? You said you'd ring.'

'Something came up,' he said. 'Something at work.'

'So you say.' She spoke in a complaining voice and Hobbs tried not to resent her tone. She didn't own him. He reasoned with her.

He said, 'I couldn't help it, Annie. It's a big case. A man's been killed.'

'A murder? A real murder?' She was impressed. She didn't take Hobbs seriously as a detective because he lived with his older married sister and looked like a schoolboy.

86

'We're still making inquiries, but — '

Annie said, 'You coming tonight? I want to see you, Billy. I missed you last night. I was feeling lonely . . . ' She lowered her voice as though someone might overhear her. 'Lonely and horny.'

'I can't help it,' he said.

'I can't help it either, the way I feel. What do you think it's like for me, all alone night after night?'

'This is a big case,' Hobbs said. 'I mean, it's not every day I get myself a murder inquiry to run.'

'You mean you're in charge?' Annie sounded doubtful.

Hobbs hesitated. He knew how she would go on and on at him about not seeing her last night, and he felt he could not bear to listen to her when she put on that hard-done-by voice.

'That's right,' he said, and he heard his voice sound strange as he told that lie. The truth was he didn't want to see Annie at the moment. He was too interested in this case, he didn't want to be distracted. He'd felt like this before when she'd made demands on him. Then he'd always tried to excuse himself with sentimental thoughts about her, as if she were a victim, which she undoubtedly was, although she was simply a victim of life, it wasn't anyone's fault. Except possibly hers, Hobbs thought, and then he was disgusted with himself. He'd been spending too much time with Sergeant Howard.

He lied again, pretending he had to go out to make further inquiries on the murder.

'I hope you don't think a murderer is going to keep you warm on a long winter's night,' she said. Hobbs knew she'd think that kind of talk would make him hot. It did but he went home just the same.

Sonia was watching television when he came in. Hobbs wished Annie could be more like Sonia. He sat down beside his sister on the settee.

'We identified the body on the mudflats,' he said.

'Who is he? We don't know him, do we?' She became anxious. 'You look as if it's someone we know.'

Sonia was not really interested in the story he was telling her. Then she heard him say the word rape.

'Rape?' she said.

'Yes, the victim was a rapist,' Hobbs said. 'The point is, because he was a rapist, as far as Sergeant Howard is concerned, it's as though he can't be a victim of crime himself.'

'You can't legislate for the way people feel,' she said.

They heard the sound of a key in the lock. Gavin came in. 'How's crime?' he asked, when he saw Hobbs.

'He's having a fine old time,' Sonia said. 'He's working on a murder.'

'I know,' Gavin said.

'How do you know?' Sonia asked.

'Talk of the ale-house,' Gavin said. 'I got a lift home and we stopped in for a quick one at The Bells.' Gavin turned to Hobbs and grinned. 'Annie came in, telling everyone how her fiancé was a hot-shot detective investigating a murder.'

'How can Bill be her fiancé?' Sonia said. 'She's already married.'

'I wasn't going to start splitting hairs with her, was I? Thank God, she didn't see me. I didn't believe her, anyway. It's true, is it?'

'It's the man who raped the Dixon girl,' Sonia said.

'The Dixon girl? I didn't think you could rape a Dixon girl.'

Sonia was indignant. 'Gavin, how could you, even as a joke? It was a horrible case.'

'Was it?' Gavin said. He opened his brief case and took out the evening paper. He sat down. 'What's for supper? Can we have it in here on our knees? I don't want to miss — '

'I know,' Sonia said. There was a detective

series Gavin liked. The hero was a mild-mannered investigator whom the villain always underestimated, but he always got his man. For some reason Gavin identified with him, but Billy said the police procedure in it was all wrong.

10

The road from the Tates' led along the brow of the headland and Marjorie drove slowly along the steep lanes looking out over the bay still glittering in the last of the evening sun. She didn't want to go home.

The thought of being alone in that echoing house appalled her. She wouldn't be able to block what she had done out of her mind. Not that she was sorry. She was consumed with anger against Tom Wheeler. She didn't care if she was being unfair. All the anger she had suppressed so long had boiled over and was directed at that man with his smug face and his perfect son and his wealth and power.

She passed the bright coloured lights of a pub garden full of a summer evening crowd. She parked the car and went in. Around her, young people were having a good time. They did not notice an overdressed middle-aged woman with smudged eye make-up and smeared lipstick. She went to the bar and bought herself a drink and then took it into the garden and sat at a small table under the strings of coloured lights.

There was a brassy blonde sitting with two

men at a table nearby. Marjorie thought she looked a little bit like Fiona when she was wearing her blonde wig, but she was bigger and much older than Fiona, and not nearly so pretty.

'He's out on a murder,' the blonde said. 'He stood me up for a corpse.'

'What corpse is that, Annie?' one of the men asked, smiling and leaning close to her.

'The one on the estuary. The one with the whip marks.'

Marjorie almost spilled her drink.

'That's what happens if you have a cop for a boyfriend,' the man said. 'But at least he's not checking on you, eh?'

'Yeah,' the blonde said, 'maybe I ought to look for some fun somewhere else.'

'You wouldn't have to look far,' the man said, drunkenly gallant, 'not someone like you.'

Marjorie felt weak. Her head was swimming. She knew she was going to faint.

When she looked up one of the barmaids was bending over her.

'Are you all right?' the barmaid asked. She helped Marjorie to her feet. Clearly the girl thought she was drunk. Everyone was staring. 'Do you need a cab?' the barmaid asked.

'No, no,' Marjorie said. 'Thank you, I'm quite all right.'

She put down her drink unfinished and left.

When she got home she rang Clem. Marjorie wanted to tell her about the woman in the pub, but she couldn't bring herself to do it.

'I went to a party tonight, but there was an incident and I left early,' Marjorie said. She couldn't tell Clem that she had hit Tom Wheeler. She'd wanted to kill him. She couldn't admit that even to herself. She went on to Clem, 'I went into a pub.'

Then she told her about the brassy blonde in the pub garden.

Clem said, 'Should I call Fiona?'

'As a matter of fact . . . ' Marjorie started to say she'd seen Fiona, but she stopped herself. 'I've already tried,' she said, 'she's out.'

Afterwards Marjorie sat in the shadowy sitting-room and thought about what happened at the Tates' party. She couldn't forget the release of hitting Tom Wheeler. He had triggered real hatred in her, and she had wanted to throttle him with her bare hands. It was tremendously exciting.

And then she'd seen Fiona and after that she'd gone into the pub and overheard that raddled blonde creature in the garden under the coloured lights and it had spoiled everything.

11

Naylor was on their trail now. They would not escape.

He was pretending to fish. He sat on the deck of the *Topsy*, a shabby little boat tied up near the *Eumenides*. The fishing line dangled into the iridescent whorls of spilled fuel beneath the pontoon. The *Topsy* was covered in rust and peeling paint. It wasn't a rich person's boat like the *Eumenides*. A passer-by seeing him would assume the ugly little tub was the sort of boat a man like himself would own, the passer-by being too stupid to see that he was a superior being.

It was still early morning and there was a chill in the air. Naylor had come to the marina straight from work and he hadn't been here long. He knew he might be all day waiting for the little blonde. She might not come to the boat that day. So, he would return tomorrow. The problem for him was that he had to go to work at night. If she came then, he would miss her. But the tides were on his side; for another week there wouldn't be enough water to get a yacht across the Bar outside the marina before

94

seven in the morning.

The water slapped the wooden slats of the pontoon. The sky looked sullen; there was a rumble of thunder in the distance. No one was taking much notice of him. A man emptying garbage bins on the pontoons told him he'd be better off fishing up-river.

'I wouldn't fancy sitting there even breathing if I was you,' the man said. Naylor ignored him. He didn't even look at the man.

No one else came near him. The boats lay at their berths, jangling and creaking among themselves. It might have been a ghost fleet.

Then he heard voices. All the time he had been sitting there he hadn't realized there was someone on board the *Eumenides*. He hadn't noticed the cabin hatch was slightly open, and the ventilator on the bulkhead had been raised. He crouched down.

There was a clatter as someone put a pan on the cooking stove in the galley. He heard the scrape of a match being struck, and the belch of gas being lit.

He got off the *Topsy* and climbed on to the deck of a motor cruiser tied up directly behind the *Eumenides*. There was an upturned dinghy on the foredeck and he squatted behind it to watch.

A few minutes later a man not much older than Naylor but already sagging from soft

95

living appeared in the *Eumenides*'s cockpit. He wore a dark suit, a shirt and tie, he was a business man, but he needed a shave. Naylor wondered if this was another sucker for Tizzy to give the whipping business to. Maybe she was playing him along preparing to get him later.

A woman's voice called, 'Sure you wouldn't like breakfast?'

Naylor knew that voice.

The man turned and leaned into the cabin entrance.

'No,' he said, 'I'd better go back to the hotel.'

Naylor saw a dark-haired woman come up on deck. She stood against the rail in the clear morning light. She didn't look the same without the blonde hair. But he knew that fluting little voice.

'Stop being so worried, Tim,' she told the man.

'I can't help it,' the man said. 'I get nervous. What if someone at the hotel says something.'

'What could they say?'

'About me not sleeping in the room,' the man said.

'They're hardly likely to say that. Why should they say a thing like that?'

'I don't know,' the man said. 'They might.'

She said, 'Trust me to get involved with a man who's afraid of his wife.'

Naylor watched as she moved to avoid the man as he tried to kiss her.

Naylor could see the man was hot for her, the way he looked at her, and then the way he had of not looking at her. Any moment now he'd start to beg her to be nice to him. She didn't bother to look at the man to see how he might be feeling. She's a bitch, Naylor thought, she didn't care what a man felt once she'd got what she wanted from him.

Then she gave the man a peck on the cheek.

The man's black leather lace-up business shoes slipped on the deck where the dew had not yet evaporated in the shadow of the cabin. He climbed clumsily over the deckrail. Naylor felt the deck under his own feet bob as the man's weight made the pontoon dip. He saw the man was going bald. His fat little arse stuck out, pushing up the flap of his coat. She'll go with anything, Naylor thought. He was jealous. He felt like he did when he was a kid and his mother went out on dates with men; that was before Mr Smith, he had never been jealous of Mr Smith and his mother. When they'd said that he was, in court, they were wrong.

The woman went below before the man

was off the boat. Naylor watched him turn to wave to her. When he found no one there, the disappointment on his face made Naylor smile. Dumb bastard, he thought. The man hurried away without turning back again.

Then Naylor saw the ventilator drop. The little tart came up out of the cabin, dressed in clothes that looked like a air-hostess's uniform. She was wearing deck shoes and carrying a pair of high-heeled sandals by the straps. As soon as she was standing on the pontoon she pulled off the deck shoes and tossed them back into the cockpit. Then she put on the high heels. She looked ridiculous as she walked carefully away from the boat, avoiding the gaps between the planks of the pontoon. Naylor had no doubts now: it was definitely her. Even if he hadn't heard that cut-glass voice he would know her. He could tell for sure now, not seeing her face, which was different without the blonde hair, but by watching the way she walked, the way she held herself and wiggled her arse. There was no mistaking her.

Naylor followed her. She walked more easily in the high heels on the concrete apron in front of the boarded-up marina shops. Naylor had to hurry to keep her in sight. She was making for the main entrance. He was thinking that at least he could see her car, even if he could not follow her when she drove out. With any luck, he thought, she would drive some flash model to go with the rest of her. He might be able to spot it around town. He would spend the day checking car parks. He was watching the movement under the tight skirt, thinking how he had got so hot watching that arse of hers move above him climbing up the ladder that night she had caused him grief. He'd give it to her all ways next time; and when she squealed, begging him to stop, he'd only give her more.

Then he heard a voice shouting, 'Hey there!'

Naylor turned. The old drunk fool nightwatchman had come out of his hut and was standing waving at him. Naylor was in a sweat. But the whore didn't turn round. She was too snotty to turn round when someone shouted in the street. Naylor swore and took one last look at her as she walked round the corner of the mall towards the car park. Then he turned and went across to the old drunk. It was a bad thing that the old fool knew him by sight and had seen him stalking the bitch. When she turned up dead the old man might put two and two together. Naylor thought he would have to deal with the nightwatchman, put Old Ted out of the way before anything happened to the little bitch. He could bang him on the head and toss him in the water some night and no one would give it a second thought when they found him drowned.

'That was your friend,' the old drunk said.

Naylor shook his head. 'No,' he said, 'not when I got close. It was someone else. I guess I'll never find her.'

He looked at the old man to see if he believed him. The old drunk smiled, as if he were going to say, 'I told you so, I knew a girl like that wouldn't have nothing to do with a scruff like you,' but he decided to keep his mouth shut.

Naylor thought, maybe I'll get him drunk until he passes out and then set him on fire. That's the way some old drunks go.

'Here,' the old man said, 'what you looking at? Who d'you think you're looking at like that?'

Naylor collected his fishing line and went home. When his mother came in she tried to make conversation but he told her to shut up, he was thinking. He was beginning to get an idea how he could make use of the little dark-haired bitch without the mess of killing her or any witnesses.

12

Marjorie, Clem and Fiona had planned some time ago to spend this weekend on *Eumenides*. They would sail if the weather was good; if not, they would give the boat a good cleaning.

When the time came, each of the women tried to find a good reason not to go. They dreaded the moment when they must meet as Megaera, Alecto and Tisiphone for the first time since they knew Martin Bakewell was dead. But there were no adequate excuses: they knew they had to face each other, and the longer they put it off, the more difficult it would be.

The wind was blowing a gale from the east. There would be no sailing unless the weather changed.

Marjorie was to pick Clem up from home. And she was late. She packed carrier bags into the boot of her car, then hurried back into the house to check she hadn't forgotten anything.

The cat, Queenie, was lying in a protected spot on the patio. Marjorie locked the cat flap. Queenie raised her head and stared at her, the wind ruffling her fur. Marjorie felt guilty. She left the transom window open over the sink in the kitchen so Queenie could get in.

On her way out she picked up a pile of letters on the mat. There was one that looked as though it might be from Ben's lawyer. He was still hassling her about the house. Now she was alone, he wanted her to sell, buy somewhere smaller and give him a share of the difference. Marjorie took the letters with her, putting them on the passenger seat of the car to look at later.

Clem lived in a rundown area off the Dock Road. It was a tedious drive across town through heavy traffic. The wind was getting stronger. It pushed people back on their heels, tossing plastic bags and pieces of filthy paper into the air.

Clem's street was a depressing row of mean red-brick dwellings. Outside in the street a ragged group of children were playing with a football between the parked cars.

Clem was standing on the doorstep looking anxiously up and down the street as though she thought Marjorie had forgotten her. As she opened the car door to get in she picked up the letters on the seat. 'What shall I do with these?' she asked.

'Oh,' Marjorie said, 'toss them in the back.'

When they reached the marina, they could barely hear themselves speak with the din of the wind rattling the boarded windows. From the pontoons they heard the groaning of fenders ground between the hulls of boats and the edge of the berths. The wind plastered Clem's short hair flat against her head. Marjorie tied her headscarf tighter under her chin.

'Fiona's here already,' Clem said. 'There's her car.' She and Marjorie exchanged smiles at the sight of Fiona's new bright red Japanese sports car.

Marjorie began to unload bags from the Deux Chevaux. The letters Clem had put on the rear seat slipped. Marjorie picked them up and put them back on the front seat.

'My God, you've brought everything but the kitchen sink,' Clem said.

'I don't think there'll be much sailing, do you?' Marjorie said. 'This is mostly cleaning stuff. I don't suppose Fiona's got much on board.'

As they came round the corner of the mall, Clem suddenly stopped. Her eyes were fixed on a little boat tied to a pontoon.

'What is it?' Marjorie asked.

Clem said, 'I could swear I've just seen him again.' She pointed towards the little tub of a boat.

'Seen who?'

'Terry Naylor.'

'It's because what's happened is making you think of him,' Marjorie said. 'You see someone who looks like him, and then you keep thinking you see him.' She was thinking of Tessa. She still thought she saw Tessa in the street sometimes. She looked across to the little boat Clem had pointed at. 'There isn't anyone there,' she said. But, seeing Clem's face, she too felt fear. Clem didn't look like someone imagining things. What if it is Naylor? Marjorie thought, and shivered.

Then Fiona was coming down the pontoon to help them with the carrier bags, and the expression on her face drove even terror of Naylor from Marjorie's mind. Fiona looked furious.

'What's happened?' Marjorie asked.

'Nothing's happened?' Fiona said. 'What should have happened?' She added, 'Nothing's wrong that the mass extermination of men wouldn't cure.'

In fact, Fiona was considerably upset. For the first time in her life, almost, she was afraid she wasn't going to get what she wanted. She was genuinely scared that she would not be able to make Bruce Wheeler want to see her again. She had to manage that if she was going to pay him back for what he'd said. 'Frank Borden's hick little secretary', he'd called her. He's not going to get away with that, she thought, I'll teach him that he can't patronize me.

There was something else, too, which made it impossible for Fiona to put that horrible little scene with Bruce Wheeler behind her. From what she'd heard, he wasn't exactly discriminating about the girls he slept with. And he'd turned her down. That, to Fiona, was a serious insult. She couldn't let that pass unavenged.

But for that she had to get together with him. This had never been a problem, with any other man. But Bruce Wheeler was in a different league from anyone she had met before. Fiona didn't at all like the feeling of not being in control. It consumed her. She had tried to ring Wheeler twice during working hours and he hadn't been there. She'd tried again that morning and this time he'd answered the telephone himself.

'You asked me to ring,' she said.

'Of course,' he said. 'I hoped you would. But I can't talk now, I'm afraid. I'm on my way out. Let me get back to you.' He put the phone down on her.

Marjorie looked at Fiona's face when she said 'the mass extermination of men', and laughed. 'Down with the lot of them,'

Marjorie said. 'I'll drink to that. There's a bottle in one of these bags.'

But there had been real malice in Marjorie's voice. Since the Tom Wheeler incident at Janet Tate's party, Marjorie had been simmering with anger against him, and against men in general. In her experience, they were all, at the very least, monsters of selfishness. But what Tom Wheeler had said to her about Tessa had been more than a slap in the face. She felt betrayed. And the sense of betrayal was growing inside her by the day, so that sometimes she thought it would choke her.

'We must've left it in the car,' Clem said.

'What?' Marjorie was miles away.

'The bottle,' Clem said. 'Let's have a quick one in the pub before we start work. I don't know about anyone else, but I could do with one.'

In the pub, Ted, the nightwatchman from the marina, was drunk in the corner and he came over when he saw them. They could scarcely make out what he was saying.

'I see you've got yourself an admirer,' he said to Fiona.

'What's he talking about?' Clem said. She shrank away from the old man. She was always afraid of scenes with drunks.

Fiona rounded on him. 'Don't speak to

106

me,' she said. 'You're drunk.' She knew what he'd said. She thought he meant Tim Yates was her admirer. She didn't want to have to explain Tim Yates to Clem and Marjorie. Tim Yates was being a pest. He said he was in love with her. He kept coming into her office and looking at her with his stupid puppy face. He had probably come to the marina to spy on her. He'd probably asked Ted about her.

The old man stood by their table, smiling at Fiona as though he'd just said a clever thing. Then he stumbled away.

'Disgusting old man,' Fiona said.

'It's not his fault he's old,' Clem said, 'young men are disgusting too.'

Fiona looked at her with amused interest. 'Young men are disgusting? What on earth's brought that on, Clem? What young man has been disgusting you?'

Clem shrugged. 'We don't all argue from the particular,' she said. 'I was making a general observation. But I can give you an example, if you want. Tom Wheeler's son, Bruce.'

There was a startled silence. Then Fiona said, 'Bruce Wheeler? What makes you think he's disgusting.'

Clem was embarrassed to be interrogated. She hadn't meant more than a conversational aside. She would have dropped the subject, but something about Fiona's combative attitude made her go on.

'A girl at work told me,' she said. 'She went out with him a few times. She got pregnant.'

'Accidentally on purpose, I suppose?' Fiona said.

Clem ignored her. 'When she told him, he tried to make her have an abortion. Then, when she wouldn't, he beat her up. I mean, really beat her up. She lost the baby. She had to spend a week in hospital.'

'She should've reported him,' Marjorie said.

'She didn't think anyone would believe her, because of his father,' Clem said. 'He was ever so sorry and paid for everything and gave her some money because she couldn't go to work. Cissie — that's her name, Cissie — forgave him. She thought they could make a go of things. He said he'd ring, but he never did.'

'She shouldn't let him get away with it,' Marjorie said.

'What did she expect?' Fiona said. 'Did she think he'd marry some little hick like her for the child's sake or something?'

'I don't know about that,' Clem said. 'The point is, she says he beat her up so she lost the child and then he paid her to keep her mouth shut. He deserves to be punished for that. You can't blame her. We don't get paid much at the Fitness Centre, you know.'

'I bet she wasn't really pregnant at all,' Fiona said. 'It probably happens a lot to a man like Bruce Wheeler.' She clenched her fists as she thought, that bastard, who consorts with the kind of cheap out-of-work models who hang round the Fitness Centre, dared to call me a hick little secretary. He turned me down.

Clem saw Fiona's face and she didn't want to argue. They went back to the boat in silence and worked until evening. The wind appeared to ease. There was a chance of a sail tomorrow. If so, they would leave at dawn.

Marjorie cooked and they drank rough Rhône wine in what seemed almost like the old camaraderie.

Then Fiona gave a deep sigh. 'It's no good, is it?' she said. 'It's there between us, even now. We've got to lay the ghost.'

She said, 'I've been thinking about what Clem said.'

Fiona poured herself another glass of wine. She looked round at the others. They seemed to be only half listening to her. 'What about a bit of fun where no one gets hurt and someone who needs to be taught a lesson gets his come-uppance?'

Fiona had no clear plan in mind. Simply,

no man — particularly no glamorous, rich and attractive man — was going to get away with treating her like trash.

'What are you on about, Fiona?' Clem asked. She grinned at Marjorie, making fun of Fiona for being drunk.

'I think we should punish Bruce Wheeler for what he did to Clem's friend,' Fiona said.

She expected a chorus of protest from the others. There was silence.

Fiona watched the two women's faces. Clem was obviously startled, then doubtful. Clem thought Fiona must be playing one of her teasing mind-games. Fiona had expected that. But Marjorie surprised her. Marjorie suddenly looked vindictive, then almost triumphant. Fiona thought, she actually likes the idea. Then she told herself, no, it's impossible, it can't be that. She's going to call my bluff.

But Marjorie didn't laugh and tell Fiona she was drunk and being silly. Marjorie had suddenly seen a way of punishing Tom Wheeler. She had some vague notion that if he thought his son was in trouble, perhaps missing for a few hours, the pompous Mr Wheeler might get some idea of what she'd felt like when Tessa disappeared. He might understand then why she was so angry at Janet Tate's party. He might see how he'd made her feel.

'Someone should do something,' Marjorie said. 'That young man is a nasty piece of work. His father's spoiled him.'

Fiona as well as Clem gaped at her.

'You're both crazy,' Clem said. She was appalled that she had started this madness, talking about Cissie.

Fiona let herself fantasize. It was her way of working out a plan. The details which made it practical came later.

'But Bruce Wheeler is different,' Clem said. 'We can't do what we did to Naylor to a man like that.'

'No, no, of course we can't,' Fiona said. 'We're only going to humiliate him a little. Just enough to make him a laughing stock if he said anything.' She thought, that'll give me something to hold over him. He couldn't dismiss me as a nobody then.

'Well, why would he agree to come with us?' Clem asked in a tone she might have used to a small child. 'Presumably this scheme of yours involves getting him to come on the boat?'

Marjorie said, 'He wouldn't come with us. He'd think he was going to seduce Fiona.' She'd been about to add 'of course', but she thought Fiona might be insulted.

But Fiona wasn't about to take offence. 'You and Clem would be hidden,' she said.

She was excited that Marjorie seemed to be serious.

'And what exactly *do* you have in mind to punish him?' Clem asked.

'I'll think of something when the time comes,' Fiona said.

There was a brief silence. Fiona picked up the almost empty wine bottle and tried to fill Clem's glass. There were only dregs left. 'He shouldn't have done what he did to your Cissie,' Fiona said.

'Let's do it,' Marjorie said.

They're both drunk, Clem thought, it's just crazy talk. Fiona's crazy, she thinks she's some kind of masked avenger, like Zoro or something. And Marjorie's as bad as Fiona. And then Clem told herself, if making plans like this helps them to lay their ghosts, it doesn't do any harm. Better let it go. Arguing about it might make them think it's real.

'Well?' Marjorie said. 'What do you say?'

13

There were Sunday church bells ringing but Hobbs didn't hear them. Sonia had been nagging him over supper last night because he hadn't provided her with the promised statistics for her talk.

He would get Sonia her figures, but that wasn't his first priority. He lay in bed wondering what he thought he was going to achieve by his avid secret study of every rape and sexual assault case in the Salthaven area over the last few years.

Hobbs pushed back the covers and got out of bed. He wanted to be out of the house before the others were up and about. As he pulled on his clothes it crossed his mind that one of the reasons he was spending so much time on the rape files was that it was an excuse not to see Annie. He was getting tired of the way she expected to come first in his life. She did not accept even murder as a good enough reason to break dates with her. But rape was different. Annie couldn't be resentful about rape as his excuse, not even if she felt it: the weight of sisterhood was too great, even for her.

Hobbs drove to the police station. Sergeant Howard had the weekend off, and with any luck Hobbs could work on the files undisturbed. But no sooner had he sat down than the telephone rang and he had a burglary to deal with.

He drove to a house in a tree-lined street in one of the older suburbs of Salthaven. An old Deux Chevaux was parked outside the front door. Automatically he checked the tax disc. Promotion to detective hadn't altogether erased old habits. He saw a pile of letters on the front seat with the name Mrs Marjorie Warren and the address. A thief would only have to see those letters while the car was parked in town and he'd know the house at that address was probably unoccupied.

Hobbs knew the name Marjorie Warren. He had read the file on the Tessa Warren case two days ago. He had seen pictures of Tessa in the files he was looking at. She looked young for her age, which was twenty-two. If he'd shown her photo to strangers and asked them to guess what she was or did, they'd think she rode horses or played tennis. They wouldn't consider the possibility of a girl who looked like that running off and disappearing, at least not of her own free will. Marjorie Warren had been in some of the pictures in the file. In the newspaper cuttings she was a weeping woman hunched with grief, a woman with frantic eyes and wild hair. As he rang the doorbell, Hobbs was careful to keep his expression sympathetic and caring.

But the woman who opened the door to him was nothing like that Marjorie Warren. She looked like an old-fashioned school matron. Hobbs decided that the woman standing in the doorway looking at him as though she'd asked a question and he hadn't answered must be another Marjorie Warren.

'Mrs Warren?'

'Yes?' Marjorie said. She held the door against the wind.

'Mrs Marjorie Warren?'

She gave him a sour look. 'If you're looking for my former husband and *that* Mrs Warren,' she said, 'you've come to the wrong place.'

'I'm a policeman.'

'Oh,' she said, 'you've got the right Mrs Warren, then. I called you.'

When she leaned over to look at his identity card, Hobbs could smell drink on her. It was early in the morning for that, he thought. Perhaps, after all, she was Tessa's mother. No one could blame her for taking to drink.

'Come in,' she said.

She led him into the living-room, and when he saw the way the place had been smashed up, although the television and video were still there, it crossed his mind that maybe there had been no burglary. A record player and tape deck were untouched, but the records, tapes and videos had been pulled out and smashed. Hobbs' policeman's mind wondered if Marjorie Warren's 'break-in' wasn't simply a drunken fight, a domestic, with some casual acquaintance she'd brought home. Drunks, he knew, got themselves into some horrendous situations. But maybe she had come home and found it like this and had had a few drinks because of it. She didn't look like a drunk, he thought. She looked too healthy, with a deep tan she certainly hadn't got out of a bottle.

'I came home from sailing,' she said, 'and found this wreckage.' Hobbs could see now that she was dressed for sailing. He asked the name of the boat. She had to spell it for him.

'There's nothing missing that I can see,' she told him. 'It's as though someone was looking for something specific. They've been through the desk and all the papers, and the clothes in my wardrobe. Even in the airing cupboard. But then they did disgusting things.'

Hobbs realized she was more distressed than he'd thought. It was more than the burglary, there was something else.

'I suppose I disturbed them coming in,' Marjorie said. 'They wouldn't expect anyone back so early on a Sunday morning. I shouldn't have been back. We were going to go sailing all weekend, but with this wind we decided against it.' Then her face clouded and she said, 'It was what he did.'

'What he did?'

'Or they did.' She was embarrassed. 'In my bed. And to my daughter's photograph.'

Hobbs asked, 'Does your daughter live here with you?' He was trying to be tactful. He still couldn't believe that this was Tessa Warren's mother.

Marjorie Warren's eyes flashed. Then she shook her head slowly. 'My daughter was Tessa Warren,' she said. 'So, no, she's not living here at the moment.'

Hobbs flushed. 'I'm sorry,' he said. 'What did they do?'

'It's so disgusting,' Marjorie said, 'I can't speak of it.' She looked away.

Hobbs went to see and when he did he didn't know what to say to the woman. He was the one who was embarrassed now. He thought maybe Sonia did have a point about some men, they behaved like animals.

In the bedroom, everything had been smashed, even a comic Mickey Mouse mask had been slashed. Hobbs noticed a box of

117

jewellery on the dressing-table. It had been overturned to lie in a jumbled heap. He thought one or two of the rings and necklaces looked valuable. He went back down the stairs to the kitchen.

'Did you leave any windows open?' he asked. 'I can't see any signs of a break-in.'

'Only the little flap one at the top in the kitchen, for the cat.'

Hobbs could see how the intruder had leaned in and opened the larger lower window to climb through. 'The back door was open when I got home,' Marjorie said. 'I'd left it bolted from the inside.'

Hobbs was losing interest. 'What time did you find it like this?' he asked.

Marjorie cast her eyes round the room as though looking for a clock to check. 'About seven, I think. We'd listened to the shipping forecast at six and decided to scrub sailing.'

'You didn't call us at once?'

Marjorie gave him a stately nod, as though conceding a point. 'Actually at first I didn't think there was much point,' she said. 'There wasn't anything missing. But things have been messed up and broken, and I thought the insurance wouldn't pay up if I hadn't reported the crime. I'm sorry.'

'You don't have to be sorry,' Hobbs said. 'You're the victim, remember.' He was impressed that she was so cool-headed. You'd almost think she expected people to treat her like this. He thought of Annie, who'd be on the phone before she got into the house if she found the back door open.

'Look,' he said to Marjorie, 'I've got to ask you this. Is there anyone with a grudge? Do you have any enemies that you know of?'

'No,' Marjorie said. 'Why should I have enemies?'

Hobbs then tried to lighten the atmosphere with some general advice on security. 'You have to watch out for little things.'

'What sort of little things?'

'Like for instance the letters on the front seat of your car.'

Marjorie was startled. 'What letters? What are you talking about?'

'I noticed on my way in. There were letters on the seat, with your address. Anyone could have seen them when you parked at the marina to go sailing. Someone could have watched you go on the boat and taken a chance on being safe here for a while.'

'My God,' Marjorie said, 'what a horrible world this is.' Her voice was flat, stating the obvious.

He said hastily, 'That doesn't mean anyone's watching you. They just see a chance and take it.'

Marjorie was thinking of how Clem thought she saw Terry Naylor at the marina, but then Clem was seeing Naylor everywhere. Before she knew what she was saying, Marjorie blurted out, 'My friend thought she saw someone watching us.'

Hobbs was alert. 'Did she? Perhaps she could give a description?'

'Oh, no, I think it was more like a shadow. She wasn't sure. That empty mall's quite spooky, you know. She was probably seeing things.'

But Marjorie could see the young policeman was excited as though he might be getting somewhere. She wished she had said nothing. At all costs she wanted Terry Naylor's name kept out of this. But she could not refuse to give Clem's name. She gave him Clem's address at the Fitness Centre as though she didn't know her well enough to have her home address.

Hobbs wrote it down. He looked at what he had written. Then it struck him. He glanced up at Marjorie, then repeated Clem's name, as though making sure he'd got it right. He had seen it in the files. She was another rape victim.

'You know her name, don't you?' Marjorie said. 'You can see why I thought she was imagining things. She still does, you know. It's only natural.'

'Yes,' Hobbs said, bowing his head in a sympathetic manner. 'Well,' he said, moving towards the front door, 'if there are any developments I'll be in touch.'

'I should think myself lucky, I suppose,' Marjorie said, 'at least there's nothing missing.'

Hobbs walked away down the drive with his head bent in the wind and sat in his car outside the house to write up his notes. He stared at the page of the notebook where he had written Clementine Illingworth's name.

Then he shut the notebook with a snap. What is this? he thought. Two women as different as that knowing each other? Even if they both like sailing, it's odd, a North Country working-class girl like Clementine Illingworth and a middle-class lady of leisure like Marjorie Warren?

There was something wrong, Hobbs was sure of it. He'd been watching Mrs Warren's face, and he was certain she'd thought of someone, that there was definitely someone she thought might have reason to break into her house and do crazy vengeful things. The break-in hadn't been a robbery. Whoever did it hadn't even bothered to make it look like one. Hobbs was puzzled. Perhaps Miss Illingworth could tell him who it was she supposed might be lurking in the shadows at the marina.

14

Naylor took off his shirt in the sun. He knew the scars were still there on his back, ugly scars, long thin ridges where the skin had sealed itself like bad stitching. The scars were shaming, a constant reminder to him that he had been mastered by three mere women, but they were now valuable. Since that body had been found, he'd only to show his back to the police and tell his story and the three women would be arrested for killing the man on the beach whose body bore the same marks. He had the women where he wanted them.

For hours he'd been sitting at the end of the pontoon pretending to fish. When he tried to stand up, his feet were numb from the cramped position. He had to sit and rub his calves to bring life back to them.

This being a weekend, and sunny, there were more people around than on a weekday. By mid-morning several families had arrived to clamber over boats tied up near him. The rush of children down the central pontoon made the wooden slats he was sitting on bob and dip so that his feet touched the water. He glared at the kids.

One small boy came up to him. He stood silently gazing at the marks on Naylor's back. Naylor ignored him, but the child would not go away. In the end, Naylor beckoned him closer and then, in a menacing whisper, threatened to throw him into the water if he didn't disappear. The boy hesitated, then looked at Naylor's face and ran off. Naylor put his shirt back on.

He moved then to sit with his precious back against the foot of *Topsy*'s stumpy mast. With his legs slightly splayed he could stretch them out straight. It was uncomfortable but he was well concealed if anyone crept up on him along the pontoon. He was afraid he might doze off. He had had no sleep. He had been on watch here all day, since early morning when he came off night watch at the factory.

There was no peace, though. The marina resounded with the din of parents and children. Naylor hated them all, but he felt good seeing how ugly they were.

There was one good-looking one though. Naylor watched her and was made uneasy. She wore denim shorts and had a little top like a baby's vest. He felt better when he saw that the girl's legs were goose-fleshed with the wind. He liked their legs white. It was more like real vulnerable flesh that way. Later in the year, when they were tanned, they lost that shared-secret quality he enjoyed. But now the girl's legs were ghostly white. He amused himself thinking what he could do to her. Almost as if she could read his mind, she stopped polishing and disappeared quickly below.

Then, bored, he watched two older, ugly women on a cabin cruiser tied up near him. The kid he had shoved away belonged to one of them. The kid came up and talked to the women but they paid no attention to him. Naylor was filled with hatred looking at the two women. He could hear them talking. They sounded like birds returned for the breeding season. If I ever marry, Naylor told himself, I'll get rid of any wife of mine who gets like that.

He thought about the three women he was hunting. Now that he was on their trail, every time Naylor thought of them he got a physical feeling, a thrill. The feeling had been very strong in the big ugly one's bedroom. He'd lain down between her sheets. I made a mess of her sheets, he thought, and then cut up her stupid mask. She'll know who did that to her.

He wondered if he had missed anything in her house. There had been nothing there. Not for him. Not much for her, either, as far as he could see. She kept no record of the past that he could find. No letters, no photograph albums. Just a few snaps of a dumpy teenage girl. She must be away from home. He'd been through her bedroom. There was a pair of homely striped pyjamas under the pillow and posters of pop stars over the bed. Naylor did not recognize them. He had pictures of Bruce Lee and Chuck Norris on his bedroom walls. He went through her chest of drawers. Her knickers were fairly fancy for a fat girl.

There had been no sign of a man in the house. The woman was very tidy; nothing seemed ever to have been used. There was only an empty dish on the kitchen floor stained with cat food. The cat was the only sign of life. He tried but he couldn't catch it. He would have liked to leave a little something as a memento. Not necessarily the whole dead cat, but maybe its head. That would've spooked her. He wanted her to know that someone with power over her had been there, someone who hated her and knew where to get her.

He might have done more but he'd heard the car, then steps outside the front door. He'd run out the back. It was only later he wished he'd stayed to watch her find the house the way he'd left it.

Then he started. Something had alerted

him. He sat up and turned so that he was kneeling, keeping low. The afternoon had faded. It was dusk. The lights along the pontoon had been switched on. On the foredeck of the *Topsy* he was below and behind the level of the lights, which were not bright, more a glow than a beam. Naylor crouched down, afraid he could be seen.

There were two people walking down the pontoon towards him, a man and a woman. Naylor recognized the woman at once. It was the one with the fancy name who called herself Tizzy. He had known it was her the moment he saw her outline and heard the click of her high heels. She wasn't dressed for sailing. The man with her leaned over to talk to her, and put out a hand to steady her when she stumbled. They stopped walking. They were just above his head now, so close that he could smell her scent. He peered above the edge of the pontoon. He could see her legs and her knees under the hem of her skirt. He could have reached out a hand and touched her leg. She was hot for the man. He was sure of that the way she was standing.

Above Naylor's head the man said, 'I was afraid I wasn't going to get away in time to make it. I'm glad you called.'

The woman hitched up her skirt and climbed over the deck rail into the cockpit.

She fiddled with a key, unlocking the hatch cover to open the cabin.

'I very nearly didn't,' she said. 'The way you behaved to me at the Tates' party, I never wanted to speak to you again.'

'So why did you?' His voice was deliberately teasing, as though he was absolutely sure of himself. Naylor expected the woman to turn round and hit him. He would've, if he'd been her. But she didn't seem to take offence. She's got a hidden agenda of some sort, Naylor thought.

'I thought I'd give you the chance to apologize,' she said. She was laughing at him. 'And, anyway, in my job I can't afford to offend potential clients. I admit I got a bit carried away at that party. I'd just been promoted. What was your excuse?'

Before he could say anything, she disappeared down the companionway into the cabin. The man jumped on board and followed her. Naylor strained to see him more clearly as he paused in the cockpit until she put on a light in the cabin. He thought he looked familiar. It was hard to be sure. The sun had gone down and the western sky glowed a bright greenish white which made it hard for Naylor to make out the details of the man's face. He thought he'd seen a man in a suit like this guy talking on TV, someone

127

important. He seemed taller and thinner than the man on TV, but how could you tell. Naylor had heard somewhere that the camera added ten pounds to everyone on the screen. Naylor smiled, thinking that the little tart probably thought she'd caught a famous man at last. She'd be after something; money, a good time, she'd definitely be after something. A little star-fucker like her was always on the lookout to see who she could get her hooks into.

The man went below. Naylor pulled himself up on to the pontoon and crept nearer. He watched as two slim hands appeared and slid the hatch cover closed. The light in the cabin blurred as she drew the curtain over the porthole. Naylor waited.

The wind had dropped. He could hear the traffic on the cliff road high above the marina. It was almost dark; he watched a car's lights far off on the foreland on the opposite side of the bay moving through the darkness, jerking and swinging like a man with a torch looking for something. Naylor did not expect the other women would come now. It looked as though the couple on the yacht were set to stay the night. He wasn't sure what to do. He found that he was shocked that a man who looked so like someone who talked on the telly could be involved with that dirty little bint.

Then the sound of the hatch cover being thrown back startled him. He crouched low. The man came up into the cockpit. Then he leaned over casually, talking back down through the hatch. 'Don't come up, sweetie,' the man said, 'I'll see myself off.'

But the woman's head and shoulders appeared. She was fully clad.

'Mr Wheeler, you're a bastard,' the woman said. 'This makes two apologies you owe me for your bad manners. Why didn't you switch off your mobile? You can't just run off on me like this.' She didn't sound angry. She was teasing him.

The man said, 'Don't you think I'd rather be here with you than listening to another of the PM's boring speeches?'

'I don't see the point in having all that power in the family if you can't do what you want for once,' she said.

'I'm really sorry,' he said. 'Why don't you finish the champagne and I'll give you a ring later?'

'Oh, forget it, what does it matter?' she said. Her tone was light-hearted, but Naylor could see she was very pissed off. The man in the suit could see it too.

'Sweetie,' he said, 'I am sorry. It's politics.'

'Not as sorry as you're going to be.'

Naylor felt like laughing and telling the

man, 'Watch out, pal, she'll kidnap you and take the skin off your back for you.'

But then she laughed. 'Forget it,' she said, 'the champagne can wait. I'm not staying. You can walk me to my car. I need things from my flat for work in the morning.'

That was bad, Naylor thought, if she stayed he could have gone aboard once it got properly dark and confronted her. He didn't have to kill her, or any of them. He could go down into the cabin and rape her, do anything, and there was nothing she could do about it, not without the police knowing who she was and what she'd done.

The light went off in the cabin. Naylor heard Tizzy pull the hatch cover shut and lock it.

'Sometime during the week?' the man said. 'Dinner? I'll leave the mobile in the car next time, I promise. We won't be disturbed by it again.'

She laughed. 'I'm a working girl,' she said, 'I can't do that. Next weekend though.'

'I'll be around,' the man in the suit said in his plummy voice. Naylor liked the idea that he would get the whip treatment. He wouldn't have minded being along to help.

'We can go for a sail on Saturday night,' the girl said. 'Just the two of us. And no one will be able to call you away.'

Naylor heard them jump on to the pontoon. They moved away from him, and he could see them at the end of the platform against the lights which had just come on in the marina mall.

Naylor didn't dare follow them to the car park across the lighted apron of the mall. He didn't want to make a mistake now. He heard her call out 'Next Saturday then' and one car door slam, then another. Naylor didn't wait to hear them drive off. His brain felt over-heated. He couldn't stand still at the stop long enough to wait for the bus. He needed to run, to walk fast, his mind was racing.

But as he came off the pontoon a policeman stepped up to him out of the shadows.

'What's this?' Naylor asked.

'That's what I wanted to ask you,' the policeman said. 'There's been a complaint.'

Naylor couldn't imagine what the man was talking about. Then he saw the two fat women and the kid from the cabin cruiser waiting on the floodlit apron of the mall.

'That's him,' one of the women said. 'He frightened the life out of the boy.'

The policeman said, 'These ladies have complained that you abused the child.'

'Abused?' Naylor said.

'Verbally,' the policeman said.

'I told him to piss off.'

One of the women said, 'He threatened to drown him.'

The kid didn't say anything but then he smiled at Naylor. 'I was only looking at your cuts,' the kid said.

'What's he mean?' the policeman said.

'I got scars,' Naylor said. 'I had my shirt off and I got scars on my back. The kid was being nosy and I'm sensitive.'

'He's got them all down his back,' the kid said. 'Big ones.'

'Can you show me some identity?' the cop asked.

Naylor showed his security guard pass.

'I see,' the policeman said. He took Naylor aside. 'Mothers are over-anxious these days,' he said. 'You can't blame them. And you know what kids are like.' He went back to talk to the women. After he talked to them Naylor saw the mother go to hit the kid, but then she thought better of it because of the cop.

'Do you have a boat here, sir?' the policeman asked Naylor.

'I was fishing.'

'Fishing?' the policeman said. 'There's no fish here.'

'So I've noticed,' Naylor said. The policeman laughed and went away.

Naylor was pleased with the way he'd handled the cop. They'd been men together, united against women and their damned kids. He went home. He had nothing else to do. He didn't like going back to that horrible poky little cottage. He resented the way his mother had come down in the world. It was as if she was out to get him.

As he came in, his mother said something to him. He didn't hear what she said. He started shouting at her anyway.

'Fuck you,' Naylor said.

He went upstairs to his bedroom and came down with a card. One of the journalists covering his court case had given it to him, telling him to get in touch if he ever wanted to make a few quid telling his story.

Naylor went to telephone. 'I'm going to do something smart at last,' he said to himself, aloud.

'What is it, darling?' his mother said, thinking he was speaking to her.

'I'm not talking to you,' he said. 'You mind your own business.'

His mother stood in the living-room doorway looking at him. She was biting her lips.

'Why must you be like this?' she asked. 'Why can't you be nice? I'm your mother.'

'This is private, do you mind,' Naylor said.

His mother closed the door. He could hear her weeping.

When Naylor got through on the phone to Barry Pearson, the journalist was angry being called at so late an hour. Naylor could tell Pearson had a woman with him. The hack didn't know who Naylor was at first. Naylor had trouble explaining what he was calling about.

'What do you mean a TV politician?' Pearson said. He sounded impatient. 'What kind of description is that?' But then the journalist laughed. 'But I don't suppose the average voter would do any better,' he said. 'A TV politician?' Barry Pearson repeated the phrase. 'Can't you do better than that?'

Naylor told him. 'He had to go see the Prime Minister. She said his name.' Naylor couldn't remember it at first. Then he said, 'It was Wheeler. She called him Mr Wheeler.'

Pearson whistled through his teeth. 'Tom Wheeler. He's the PM's top adviser. He's worth billions.'

'He said he had to be somewhere with the PM. The tart didn't like that.'

'What's she after?'

Naylor said, 'It's a set up. That tart is setting him up.'

'Steady on,' Pearson said. 'The upright Tom Wheeler with his pants down with a young girl is good enough for me. We don't have to get carried away. You know who this guy is, don't you?'

'No, I don't. I don't vote,' Naylor said. 'Why should I make some guy rich and famous?'

15

Hobbs was working on the computer when the uniformed cops were coming in off their shift. Greene, one of the men he'd been with on Traffic before his promotion, came over and asked why didn't Hobbs come out for a farewell beer with him. Greene was going away. He was leaving the Force. He had a brother with a central-heating repair business in Canada and he was leaving to join him. It was his last night and he was standing the boys drinks in the pub.

'I'll come and have one with you,' Hobbs said.

He was about to log off the computer when Greene looked at the screen and said, 'I saw him today.'

'Who?'

'Him,' Greene said. He pointed at the picture on the screen. 'There was a complaint about him shouting at a kid. Maybe I should've questioned him more, but after all it's my last day on the job. I didn't know he was on the books.'

'What was he doing?'

'He said he was fishing. Down in the

marina, can you believe? He scared a kid who was pestering him and then the kid's mother and aunty complained to me. Naylor said he had his shirt off and the kid was looking at some scars he'd got and your man didn't like that. He said he was sensitive about them. The kid said there were cuts on his back.'

'Where in the marina was he fishing?'

Greene shrugged. 'I told him there weren't any fish, but you'd think he'd know that for himself. He came off an old tub called the *Topsy.*'

Hobbs had a beer with Greene in the pub, with everyone saying they wished they had a brother in Canada with a central-heating repair business they could go into and make some real money. Hobbs said so too.

Then he drove to the marina. He walked along the pontoon. He wasn't the only person out taking the night air, but no one else was alone. Hobbs felt quite conspicuous being on his own. He tried to look as though he had somewhere definite to go.

Then he saw the *Topsy* and close by he saw the *Eumenides.* He knew the name of that boat. That was the yacht Mrs Warren said she and Clementine Illingworth sailed with Fiona Farr.

Hobbs had already checked out Fiona Farr. She was not a rape victim. According to the records, she had never even been assaulted. But a man had once brought an assault charge against her. The charge should probably have been wiped from the files by now but it was still there. The man had called the police and said she attacked him and she'd been taken to court. But in court the man had dropped the charges. That was four years ago. She'd done well for herself if she owned a boat like the *Eumenides*.

They were a strange trio, Hobbs thought, those three women. Fiona Farr had shown she could be violent, while the other two were victims of violence. Then Terry Naylor, apparently, had scars on his back which weren't there when he was in custody, not according to the files, they weren't recorded as distinguishing marks. He'd got them since then. Hobbs wondered what kind of scars they were. He wondered if they could possibly be the marks of a whipping. A thought occurred to Hobbs but he pushed it aside. He couldn't see Mrs Warren being violent. It was too preposterous.

16

Clem was in a panic. There was someone in the room with her. She felt a hand over her mouth. She woke, trying to scream. It was another rape dream. She had them regularly. She thought they'd go away with time, but they didn't. It was worse when she was alone. There was supposed to be another girl who lived in the house with her, a colleague from the Fitness Centre, but she was always at her boyfriend's.

Lying in bed, wide awake now and knowing that she was safe, Clem nevertheless felt anxious. It was always the same after the nightmares. She was frightened of the future. It seemed to her that the rest of her life she was going to be quite helpless to change the bad things which were waiting to happen to her. What do I have to live for? she asked herself, and then she thought, I'm not alive; I'm not living at all.

Naylor hadn't just raped her and left her with nightmares which still made her scared to go to sleep at night. What happened had poisoned everything in her life. She had dropped out of university because she couldn't face the other students. They knew what had happened to her. It was common knowledge on the campus. When Naylor was brought to court and then released, she was sure the other students would assume she'd made up the allegations against him out of some perverted spite. What else could they think, after all?

Sometimes she even wondered if she had. She was haunted by the way the jury and the judge had looked at her, not believing her. Did she accuse the wrong man? How could she be so sure her attacker was Naylor?

No, she was certain, no doubts at all. But she had failed to convince those people in court that she had told the truth. They had found her wanting in some way. Clem was ashamed, and confused.

She pulled the duvet up to cover her face. She was suddenly homesick. She was filled with longing for her mother, for her quiet father in his chair by the fire, for the warm damp smell of the kitchen when it was raining. The pain stabbed like a knife in the heart. Oh, Mum, she said to herself.

They'd been so proud of her, she couldn't bear them to know that she had destroyed their hopes. She'd never even told them she'd been raped. Her parents were older than most other people's her age. Her father was more like a grandfather. They'd never talked to her about sex. They'd have been embarrassed if she'd tried to tell them what Terry Naylor had done to her. She thought they'd think she'd done something to lead him on. They knew as well as she did that she wasn't obviously sexy, or even attractive. The way she'd been at the time, if they'd asked her almost anything, she'd have thought they were accusing her.

Clem heard the clatter of milk bottles from further up the street. Her hands were trembling. She wasn't going to stay here alone another night. She dressed and then she packed her clothes and a few personal belongings into a rucksack and strapped it on to the carrier of her bicycle. She did not know where she would go but she didn't want to stay alone any more.

The Fitness Centre was already open. Several regulars came in from six each morning to work out before going to the office. Clem warmed up and ran through a few simple routines before going across to work on the weights. She wanted to make her body sweat and hurt, to force the tension out of it. It was no use; it didn't help.

All day she worked her clients harder than usual. She was like a robot, unsmiling, absorbed, pressuring them, not even bothering to hide her impatience when they could do no more. Cissie was watching her.

'If you don't let up on them,' Cissie said, 'there'll be complaints.'

'So let them complain,' Clem said. 'They're the ones who want to get fit. Do they expect me to do it for them?' She thought for a moment she might ask Cissie to let her stay over with her, but Cissie was another girl who was never at home.

Early in the afternoon Clem was told she had a visitor and she went to reception and there was a young man waiting.

'I'm sorry to bother you at work,' he said. 'I'm DC Hobbs.' He showed his identity, which she ignored. She was shaking. She was afraid he would see her hands trembling if she took his warrant card to look at. 'We're making inquiries about a break-in at Mrs Warren's,' he said.

'At Marjorie's? Is she all right?'

'It seems the thief didn't get away with anything. But we think it happened when the intruder knew she was away. She mentioned you saw someone hanging about at the marina.'

'Oh, that was just my imagination,' Clem said. 'Marjorie didn't see anyone, and I can't be sure I did. In fact, I'm sure I didn't, really.'

Clem could see Cissie standing smiling looking at her talking with a young man. Men

142

came to the gym to take the other girls who worked there on dates, but this was the first time a young man had come to the gym to see Clem.

'Is there somewhere we can talk?' Hobbs asked.

She took him to the room where they did the accounts.

'I don't want to get you worried,' he said, 'but do you know a man named Terence Charles Naylor?'

It was like court again hearing a man called by three names. They'd recited Naylor's three names in court.

Hobbs fumbled in his breast pocket and brought out a photograph.

'Is this the man?' he said.

There was Naylor looking out at her. It was terrible seeing a picture of Terry Naylor and being asked if she had seen him.

'He's the man who raped me,' she said. 'What are you trying to do to me?'

'You haven't seen him recently, have you? In the last few days?'

'No.'

She knew Hobbs could see how nervous she was. He offered her a cigarette. She said she didn't smoke and he said he didn't either but he always carried a packet in case there was an accident or robbery and the person he was talking to was nervous.

She said, 'Has he done it again?'

'Done what?' Hobbs asked.

'He's done something criminal, hasn't he?' she said. 'Why else would you show me his picture?'

Her voice was shaking. She took a deep breath. She was fighting back tears.

'Could this be the man you saw at the marina?' Hobbs asked.

'I told you, I don't even know if I saw anyone. I see shadows everywhere.'

'I'm sorry,' Hobbs said. He knew he should press home his questions, but he couldn't do it. 'I'm sorry,' he said again.

When he was gone Cissie came up to Clem and said, 'I liked your boyfriend. He's cute.'

'He's not my boyfriend,' Clem said.

'He'd like to be,' Cissie said. 'I saw the way he was looking at you.'

Clem didn't tell Cissie that Hobbs was the police.

Later in the evening, Marjorie came in to do a few circuits. She thought Clem looked pale and ill, but decided against saying anything about it.

Clem asked about the robbery.

'So you've talked to the police?' Marjorie asked.

Clem nodded. She didn't mention that the

young constable had showed her Terry Naylor's picture.

Clem put a hand on Marjorie's arm and said, 'You've got a spare room, haven't you, Marjorie? Can I stay with you for a bit?'

She looked so anxious that Marjorie couldn't say no. But she wanted to refuse. More than burglars, she was frightened of having someone else in the house. I don't want to get to like the company, she thought. If I get to like it, she'll leave me. Like Ben did, and Peter, and Tessa. Marjorie was very conscious that no one, until the intruder and the young policeman, had been upstairs in her house since Tessa had disappeared. Clem couldn't have Tessa's room, that was impossible. There were other rooms. But Marjorie was afraid. She opened her mouth to make an excuse but then she said:

'Of course you can. It'll do me good to have the company.'

17

The pile of computer print-outs on Hobbs's desk grew larger. The world was full of madmen. And he was falling behind on what some of his colleagues were calling his day job. He had not written up the paperwork on cases dealt with days ago. He had not done his expenses. He knew he must get these signed quickly, or he was going to be overdrawn on his account at the bank. There was just no time.

Hobbs had told Sergeant Howard he was going through the rape files for Sonia. The sergeant had a soft spot for Sonia. He didn't suspect that Hobbs had an ulterior motive. As far as Sergeant Howard was concerned the Martin Bakewell business was closed. The coroner had returned a verdict of death by misadventure. Sergeant Howard had not wavered in his view that the young man had committed suicide. If anything, the sergeant was pleased about it. It was appropriate that Bakewell had a guilty conscience and that after his spell on remand in prison he killed himself. In Sergeant Howard's view it showed that the system worked.

Hobbs knew that if he told Sergeant Howard of his theory about vigilantes, his superior wouldn't be at all pleased. And ordinary vigilantes would be bad enough, let alone female vigilantes who kidnapped rapists, flogged them and then threw them into the sea. Especially, he wouldn't be pleased when Hobbs told him that one of those vigilantes was Mrs Marjorie Warren, whose ex-husband was Ben Warren, a former member of Salthaven City Council and still a member of the Police Commission. It would be a huge scandal if a woman like Ben Warren's ex-wife was dishing out vigilante punishment to sex offenders. The sergeant had some odd views on crime and punishment, but he would find that too much to take in. Yet there were precedents: there were several cases of vigilantes around the country. Hobbs hadn't realized how many himself until he broadened his search of the files and started looking at cases all over England and Wales. Many ordinary people were taking the law into their own hands these days. There was a definite trend. Hobbs knew that crimes ran in cycles and vigilantes were in fashion.

Even so, Hobbs himself had difficulty believing his own theory about Mrs Warren. He told himself that she might've been unhinged by her daughter's disappearance.

But Hobbs puzzled how a woman like Marjorie Warren would ever have the nerve to do more than talk about taking revenge on rapists. She might campaign for her Women's Institute branch to propose a resolution for the Annual Conference that sex offenders be summarily castrated, but surely that was about the limit.

Hobbs had another problem, and that was with Terry Naylor. Naylor came from a nice middle-class background, but he was a thug just the same. If Naylor had been the victim of vigilantes, he would want revenge. He would blame Clementine Illingworth. Neither Marjorie Warren nor Fiona Farr was connected to him, as far as Hobbs could discover. Why would he break into Marjorie Warren's house and defile her daughter's bed? How would Naylor know that Miss Illingworth had ever met Mrs Warren? Surely any vigilante group would wear some sort of disguise. Then he thought of the Mickey Mouse mask he'd seen slashed to pieces at Mrs Warren's, and he wondered.

As for Clementine Illingworth, Hobbs felt quite angry that anyone should suggest she could ever be such a thing as a vigilante, although no one except himself had done anything of the kind. She was still terrified of Naylor. Hobbs had seen her hands trembling.

But if Naylor had been attacked . . . There was the boy at the marina talking about marks on Naylor's back. They could have been anything. But why was Naylor fishing at the marina? There were no fish there. Naylor had been born in Salthaven and everyone in Salthaven knew that there were no fish in the marina. But the boat, the *Eumenides*, was berthed where Naylor was fishing. It was an odd coincidence. But, Hobbs told himself, when you're a detective you have to stop believing in coincidences. If Naylor had been attacked, and knew who had attacked him, he was the type who'd hunt them down. And do what? Something horrible. Hobbs thought of Clementine Illingworth being attacked by Naylor. Then he tried to think of Clementine Illingworth attacking Naylor. It was hard to believe, as hard as imagining Mrs Warren doing it. Both women were physically strong, but they weren't tough mentally, not after what they'd been through, and who could blame them? There must be someone else, he thought. The Farr woman? It was her boat.

Hobbs hadn't seen Fiona Farr, but from what he'd read in her file, he thought that if the three of them were involved in anything, she'd be the driving force, whoever she was. Hobbs wondered what excuse he could make to see her.

The telephone rang. It was Annie. Hobbs's heart sank.

'You're late, Bill,' she said. 'You said you'd pick me up.' She was annoyed. She spoke in a particularly shrill voice.

He said, 'I can't tonight.'

He heard her catch her breath and waited for the explosion.

'Where do you think you get off, treating me like a piece of shit? Tell me that.' She paused but he said nothing. She spoke in a more reasonable voice. 'I'm not something you can pick up and use and throw away when you feel like it.'

Hobbs couldn't argue with her. He tried to appease her. 'Annie, it isn't that I don't want to see you. I just can't at the moment. It's my job.'

'Bugger your sodding job,' she screamed at him. Then she said in a calm voice, 'I want you to know I'm not waiting around, I'll get myself a proper man.'

Hobbs took a deep breath. This was his chance. He kept his voice low and even. 'Yes,' he said, 'I understand. I'd never try to stop you. I want you to be happy.' He sounded phoney even to himself. He'd lost all sympathy for her. Perhaps he'd lost it a long time ago. She'd probably known before he did. They had intuition, women did. Sonia often knew things by some kind of instinctive process he didn't have at all.

'Happy?' she said. 'You want me to be frigging happy? That's a good one. When did you ever do anything to make me happy?' She was screeching again.

'There's nothing I can do, is there?' he said.

She was not quite sure of herself now. 'Well, I'm going out anyway,' she said. 'I want some fun. I've a right to some fun, haven't I?'

'Yes,' he said wearily, 'I wouldn't want to stop you.'

'You wouldn't say that if you loved me,' she said. 'You wouldn't want me to go out. You'd never want me to be happy except with you. There's no point in us when we don't see each other for days on end.' She was working herself up again. 'It's over, you know that? You know what I'm saying?'

'Yes,' he said, 'I guess that's that.'

'You fucking bastard,' she said. She put the phone down.

Hobbs felt guilty at how relieved he was. Because he felt guilty he knew he wouldn't be able to refuse to see her again if she called him. He didn't understand women. Sonia had told him that often enough. She was always warning him about them taking advantage of him because of it. And Annie was always saying it, too; she was constantly blaming him for being insensitive to her woman's needs. And here he was trying to understand complicated women like Mrs Warren and Clementine Illingworth in order to make some sort of case against them. He thought, I'm out of my depth, I'd better forget it.

He didn't want to go home. He drove out of town, up the hill behind Salthaven where big broken-down Victorian houses stood looking out across the sea. They were haunted houses, Hobbs thought, full of ghosts, haunted houses hidden by tangles of overgrown laurel and rhododendron. Most of them had been converted into flats. Fiona Farr lived in one of them. He thought there was no harm in taking a look.

She lived in one of the better conversions. Hobbs stopped the car and took out a police leaflet on security. It would be enough of an excuse if she wasn't suspicious, and if she was suspicious he was on to something.

When the girl came down to answer the door he thought he must have pushed the wrong bell. She looked like a teenager, in a sweatshirt, her glossy black hair in a pony tail, and denim shorts showing off deeply tanned legs.

'I'm looking for Miss Farr,' he said.

'That's me.' She didn't ask who he was, and stepped back to let him into the hall. He had to make a special effort to make her look at his police identification. She seemed to have no idea of the danger a young woman living on her own could be in. He could see up the stairs the open door of her flat. Music came from it. 'It's not a party,' she said, 'I'm cleaning up. I like to have a lot of noise when I'm doing housework, and pretend it's fun.'

He followed her up the stairs and only when she had shut the door of her flat behind him did she ask, 'Have I done something wrong?'

'It's a security matter,' he said. He handed her the pamphlet. He could have done that downstairs but she didn't seem to mind. He supposed she was bored doing the cleaning, even with the loud music, and welcomed any diversion. 'It's your boat,' he said. 'We're having a security drive. There've been some robberies from boats at the marina.'

'Actually, it's not my boat,' she said. 'It belongs to a man I used to know. I mean, I still know him, but he's gone away. I just act as if it's mine.' She walked across the room to turn off the radio. 'Would you like a drink?' she asked. 'Housework makes me thirsty.'

Hobbs had a drink.

The young woman — he could see now she

was a young woman and not a teenage girl
— was very attractive, very charming in a
friendly, almost professional, way. Hobbs
wasn't sure himself what he meant by that. It
was as though the easy, friendly manner she
had was contrived, like a celebrity's smile.
Perhaps it was just the way ambitious
professional women were, so sure of themselves. He had no doubt she was an ambitious
professional woman. He corrected himself, an
ambitious career woman. Still, he couldn't
stop looking at her, and he couldn't imagine
her leading Clementine Illingworth and Mrs
Warren into a life of crime. But then, he
couldn't imagine her smashing up a man's
flat. Or maybe he could. Maybe she'd loved
the fellow and that was the only way of
getting his attention. Anyway, she sat on the
arm of a sofa and Hobbs had never seen
anything prettier than the way she smiled at
him. She knows, he thought, she knows I'm
standing here thinking how pretty she is. She
thinks all she'd have to do is snap her fingers.
And then he thought, she'd eat me alive.

'Do you like this flat?' she suddenly said.
'Don't you think it's a bit creepy? I know
there's the big window, but it sometimes gives
me the creeps. It's those fir trees and the
apocalyptic sunsets.'

Hobbs wasn't going to tell her that as a kid

he'd always thought the houses along this road were haunted. He walked across the room to look out of the bay window. Studholme Island looked very black against the glittering sea. He used to think wicked wizards lived on Studholme Island, among the seagulls. He turned back into the room and said, 'What about the boat? Do you ever get the creeps on the boat?'

She laughed. Hobbs laughed too. She was the most uncreepy person he'd ever met, even in this flat. There was something about her, some suppressed energy, which was very attractive, more than just her looks.

'Do you sail alone?' he asked. 'It's a big boat.'

'A thirty-footer. I can handle her alone. But I've got two friends, two girlfriends, who crew for me. Well, not friends, really, except for sailing. We're an unlikely trio, except we all love sailing.'

Does she know I've talked to the other two? Hobbs thought. Was it really possible? Those three women taking men like Naylor and Bakewell and flogging them? It wasn't likely, but with women anything was possible. Women were odd. There was some odd strength about female relationships. They talked about sisterhood. When Hobbs thought of the word sisterhood he thought of Sonia. Of course he wanted to protect Sonia because she was his sister. But women's friendships weren't like the camaraderie of the lads at the station. The lads all liked a pint after work to talk about football, but women didn't seem to need booze, or sport, to bring them together. The fact of being women seemed to be enough for them. The only connection he could see between those three women was membership of the sisterhood. Was that enough to turn them into vigilantes?

18

Clementine Illingworth wouldn't have looked as scared as she had, Hobbs thought, not if she'd been looking at someone she hadn't seen since the court case. At least, she wouldn't have looked scared in quite the way she did. She'd be looking at someone she'd once feared, true, but when he showed her Naylor's picture, he'd been certain she felt under actual and immediate threat. She wasn't the sort of girl who could cover up her feelings. He'd thought she looked very attractive coming out from the office at the back of the gym and then she saw him and her face had dropped. It was bad having that effect on a pretty girl but it often happened. He hoped it was only because he was a policeman.

Hobbs was thinking of Clementine Illingworth as he drove to work. Then he saw her. She was pedalling through the rain on her bicycle. He followed her down the wet street. The rain lashed the road. Hail drummed on the car roof. He saw her get off her bicycle and wheel it across the pavement into a pub. He parked his car and followed her inside.

She was sitting at a table in the corner drinking orange juice.

'Miss Illingworth?' he said, as if he weren't sure it was her.

She looked startled. He could tell she was nervous of the police. 'What are you doing here?' she asked.

'Taking refuge from the rain,' he said.

She smiled and he pulled a chair over and sat down. She was a very pretty girl when she smiled but he supposed she didn't smile often and when she wasn't smiling Hobbs thought how terribly sad she looked. He'd seen a photograph of her in the files from the time before it happened and then she had not been sad like that. Clementine Illingworth had been a nice, straightforward, cheerful girl until that thing happened to her.

To try to put her at ease, he told her some funny stories about life at the police station and she smiled and once she laughed out loud. Then she said, 'This rain's not going to stop. I'll have to risk it.'

'I'll give you a lift,' he said. 'We can put your bike in the back. I can tie the tailgate down.'

'Isn't it out of your way?'

'It doesn't matter.'

'Aren't you on duty?'

'Not yet. My shift starts later.'

In the car she looked out at the wet streets. 'Towns are ugly in the rain,' she said.

'There's some nice country round Salt-haven. Out where my sister lives is nice.' Then he said, 'I live with my sister and her husband.'

'I was brought up in Yorkshire,' she said, 'the dales where I lived were nice.'

'Maybe you should get out for a walk in the hills round here,' Hobbs said.

'Maybe I should,' she said.

When Hobbs dropped her off he drove away thinking, I didn't have to ask her about herself. I didn't have to ask her anything. I've got a file on her. I've got colour photographs of her face bashed in and her breasts and thighs all covered in blood and black and blue with bruises. I know all about her.

But she was holding something back. Hobbs was sure of it. It crossed his mind that she might be afraid because Naylor had found her and was harassing her. He was the sort who might well threaten her. She wouldn't go to the authorities again, not after what happened before.

Of course, Hobbs thought, the last thing she wants is a cop coming round showing her photos of rapists. She wouldn't want anything at all to do with any of it. Or would she? Clementine Illingworth might be like Fiona

Farr; she might suddenly become angry like Miss Farr was capable of being. And if Clementine Illingworth did get into a fury about rapists, was that unnatural? Wasn't it possible that if Naylor were blackmailing her, or threatening her, she'd be driven to do something about it? Maybe it would be for the best if someone took Terry Naylor out one night and drowned him.

19

Clem had already been several days at Marjorie's but no one could say she filled the house with the joys of youth.

She showed no interest in anything Marjorie suggested. It was Sunday, but the girl had shut herself in her bedroom most of the morning. In the end Marjorie, exasperated, knocked on the door and proposed going out for lunch. Clem refused.

So Marjorie ate Sunday lunch alone and all she wanted to do was talk, to talk about anything as long as someone said something in return. Damn, she told herself, I was afraid of this. I'm trying to make her need me. And then she thought, no, I'm already beginning to need her.

The sudden ringing of the telephone made her start. Marjorie dropped the cup of coffee. Scalding liquid started to drip on to the floor. But Marjorie belonged to the generation where a ringing telephone must be answered, whatever the distractions.

'Hello, yes?' she said.

'Marjorie?' Fiona sounded surprised at the brusqueness of Marjorie's tone.

'Fiona? I'm sorry, I've a small domestic crisis. Is something wrong?'

'Wrong? Why should anything be wrong? No, it's good news. Tonight's the night. You know what to do.'

Fiona put the phone down.

Marjorie sat down at the kitchen table and watched the coffee dripping on to her precious quarry tiles. Oh, God, she thought, what have I got myself into now?

It had been so different when they were all together on the boat, that night they'd planned the excursion which would give Bruce Wheeler a bit of a scare; and jolt his father out of his complacency. On the boat, on their second bottle of wine, it had all seemed so simple. They'd planned it down to the last detail. Clem would be on board from the start, hiding in the sail locker. But there wouldn't be room for Marjorie. So she'd drive to an isolated cove where the foreshore was within quite easy rowing distance of a stony beach on Studholme Island's landward shore. Marjorie would inflate the rubber dinghy, and then, at a signal from Clem, row out to where the *Eumenides* was anchored close to the island. The three of them would then strip Bruce Wheeler, force him into the dinghy, and abandon him naked on the island. It didn't amount to much of a punishment, perhaps, but it would be humiliating. There was a chance he might think twice about his abusive ways with women in future.

Marjorie had wondered at the time what Fiona, once she sobered up, would expect to gain from their venture. Bruce Wheeler wouldn't know who Marjorie and Clem were, but he did know who Fiona was. And yet she'd scoffed at the idea of disguise. She'd said that Bruce Wheeler would only agree to the sailing trip if he thought he could fuck her — that was the word Fiona used, and though Marjorie didn't like it, that was the way young women talked. Fiona was taking a tremendous risk. She's probably got an ulterior motive of her own, Marjorie thought.

Their idea was that one of the regular tourist boat trips which regularly dropped in on Studholme would be bound to rescue Bruce Wheeler within a few hours. He wouldn't be physically harmed, but he'd be a laughing stock. And whatever story he came up with to explain his predicament, he was never going to admit what really happened. He would never live that down. At best, he might get some idea of what it felt like to be a sex object. It didn't occur to Marjorie to think that she herself didn't know what it felt like to be a sex object. She knew a lot of women did, and she would take their word for it that it was a bad thing.

They were going to have a bit of fun with Bruce Wheeler, that was all. As far as Marjorie was concerned it had been a game to pass the time on a windy night when they couldn't sail and had had too much to drink.

Now Fiona had suddenly announced 'Tonight's the night!' as though the whole thing was a *fait accompli*. Marjorie realized what she had agreed to do. She thought, I never agreed. But she hadn't refused, and now it was too late to back out even if she wanted to. And then she remembered Tom Wheeler's careless words about Tessa at the Tates' party. 'Am I crazy?' she said aloud.

Marjorie suddenly became aware that Clem was watching her. The girl was standing in the doorway, looking at her with a little smile on her face. Marjorie thought, how long has she been there? She said, 'That was Fiona on the phone.'

'So tonight's the night?'

Marjorie raised her head to look out of the open window. It was a pleasant evening. There was the sound of birds in the garden. It was peaceful. No night for an act of vengeance. She turned to look at the sulky young woman. Clem was not like Tessa. Tessa might lose her temper but then it was all over.

Clem was sulky like Peter had been sulky. Marjorie had always been able to get Tessa out of one of her moods with an outing, or a shopping trip, but nothing would take Peter out of a sulk.

Then Clem grinned and Marjorie was disarmed.

'Relax,' Clem said. 'You're nervous. I'm nervous. That's all.'

'Are you nervous?'

'Of course I am,' Clem said.

'Would you like something to eat?' Marjorie asked. Clem laughed. Suddenly Marjorie heard herself as she must sound to Clem and she, too, smiled.

Clem, in her blunt Northern voice, said, 'You don't have to worry about me, Marjorie. Stop fussing. You know, your trouble is, you've forgotten how to be friends with someone.'

Marjorie turned to look at her. 'Is that what we are, friends?' she asked.

'Well, yes. Aren't we?'

'But we don't know each other.'

'We trust each other. How could we do the things we've done together if we didn't trust each other? We've been there for each other.'

Marjorie was embarrassed by the emotion in Clem's voice. I'm no good at this, she thought. She turned her back again to look

165

out of the window.

'And I don't think I even like Fiona that much,' Marjorie said. 'Can you not like a friend?'

Clem hesitated for a moment, and then she said, 'You don't have to like Fiona. You disapprove of her. I disapprove of her, too. I'm afraid of her. But I'd like to be more like her. She's not afraid to be self-centred. God, what I couldn't do if I was self-centred like that.'

'But is she a friend?'

'She's proved it, hasn't she. So've you. Friends look after each other. Like you and I have.'

'But I couldn't . . . well, confide in you. I couldn't talk about myself.'

'You mean you wouldn't,' Clem said.

There was that overpowering emotion again in the room, stronger than the scent of the nicotiana growing wild outside the window. Marjorie was still standing with her back to Clem, staring out at her unweeded garden.

'I thought Tessa was the best friend I've ever had. And she's gone, and now I wonder if she wasn't a complete stranger.'

'What are you saying?' Clem could only see Marjorie's broad back and slightly hunched shoulders as she stood staring into the garden.

'I wish I'd done things differently,' Marjorie said. Clem had to strain to hear her. Marjorie went on, 'I've used Tessa as an excuse, haven't I? But after my husband left . . . ' She stopped. 'I'm going to make tea,' she said. 'Do you want a cup of tea at least?'

Clem thought, I should tell her I think this whole thing is crazy, that we should tell Fiona we're not going to do it.

Marjorie went into the kitchen. The chance had been missed. She'd been going to tell Clem she didn't want anything more to do with Fiona, and then the moment had gone when she could've said she didn't want to go on with their plan to humiliate Tom Wheeler's son. She filled the kettle. She put tea bags in two mugs. She took the milk out of the fridge. It struck her suddenly that it might possibly be because of Ben that she had clung on to the memory of Tessa as she had. As long as she kept their daughter enshrined, she still had a part of Ben. Surely not? That couldn't be true. She felt shocked, much as she did after she caught sight of herself reflected in shop windows; a horrified and helpless recognition. She told herself, I wanted to use what happened to get him back. I thought he'd feel sorry for me. I even got fat so he'd feel sorry for me. I thought it would matter more to him to be needed than to be happy.

The kettle boiled. Marjorie ignored it. She was deep in thought. Ben went with Nathalie because he wanted to be happy. Why don't I know how important being happy is? I don't think I know what it means.

The kettle continued boiling while Marjorie stood there. She thought, does my life really count? A helpless, unimportant middle-aged, self-deluded, woman, what does it really matter? I'm not happy. And I haven't the least idea of how to make one single other person in the world happy. I can care for them, like I'm beginning to care for Clem, but that's a kind of emotional imprisonment for them. Then she thought, Fiona knows how to be happy. She does what she wants, she doesn't just wait for things to happen to her. As she thought of Fiona, curiously, Marjorie felt less anxious. She trusted Fiona, in a way, just because she was too self-centred to let anything get out of control and threaten her. Then at last Marjorie saw the kettle boiling.

She took the mug of tea to Clem. 'I'll take you down to the marina when it's time,' she said.

Clem sat drinking the tea. She didn't seem to have a word to say, and Marjorie didn't want to talk now. She was tired, and her head had begun to ache. At last, she looked at her watch and said, 'It's time to go. I'll get the car out. You get your gear.'

Clem said, 'Stop fussing.'

'Right,' Marjorie said. 'I'll drop you and come back here until it's time for me to go to the cove and do my stuff with the dinghy. And the pump. What if I can't work the pump?'

Clem laughed. 'You'll work the pump all right,' she said. 'Don't worry about the pump.'

Marjorie said, 'When you come in the boat it'll be dark, how am I going to know when you've anchored?'

'You'll see our lights. The lights will be there.'

Clem was matter of fact. Marjorie felt elderly and dithering. She said, 'A light could be anyone.'

'OK,' Clem said, 'I'll flash the torch from the forehatch. Three short flashes, right? I should be able to manage that. They'll be below.'

'Right,' Marjorie said, 'I'll start rowing out as soon as I see that. And once I'm on board, we do our stuff.'

'There should be something to see by then,' Clem said. She laughed, but Marjorie didn't. She didn't want to think about Bruce

169

Wheeler making love to Fiona.

They were both silent as Marjorie drove to the marina. It had been a fine evening, and a number of elderly couples were strolling along the promenade in the balmy twilight. Marjorie thought they looked like she had imagined she and Ben would look when they got old. Everything in the twilight looked so normal, she couldn't believe what she was about to do. She imagined Ben's face if she told him; it made things seem a little less daunting.

At the marina, Marjorie got out of the car and walked with Clem to the head of the pontoon. The sun was setting behind the foreland.

'Good luck,' Marjorie said.

'You too,' Clem said.

Marjorie turned and walked back to the car. At the edge of the mall, she looked back. There was no sign of anyone. Her head was pounding.

When she arrived home it was still some hours before she had to start for the cove and wait for the boat. She made coffee. She kept looking at the clock but each time she did only seconds had passed. There was a nagging, jagged pain behind her left eye. She sipped the coffee. She could not swallow it. She thought she was going to vomit.

'I'm getting a migraine,' she said to Queenie. It was some time since she had last had an attack. 'Why now?' she said, but she didn't need Queenie to give her the answer.

And then it seemed the perfect excuse. If she was sick she couldn't go to the cove. She couldn't pump up the rubber dinghy and row out to the boat. Now she did feel sick, it was the truth. She had an acid taste at the back of her throat. She leaned over the sink, feeling her stomach heave. She lay down on the settee in the drawing-room. The pain in her head swelled and gripped. She looked at her watch again. There was still two hours to go. But I can't let the others down, she thought. They're relying on me. Fiona knows what she's doing, Marjorie told herself, she knows how to handle a man. She never loses control with men. She said so herself. She's always boasting about it. And Clem'll be there. No man's going to hurt Fiona with Clem there watching.

Marjorie got up from the settee and went up the stairs, bent over like an old woman. She took a pill and lay down on the bed in the dark. She could see the clock on the table. She had time. She would see how she felt later. She would decide then. But she could not think for the pain. She had to close her eyes.

20

Hobbs tried to concentrate on his expenses. But every time he looked at the figures in front of him, he saw Clementine Illingworth's brief sad smile instead. He tried to think of some excuse for seeing her again. But she wouldn't want to see him. He knew that. He couldn't get out of his head the look she'd had on her face in the pub when she'd glanced up and seen him standing in front of her.

Sergeant Howard came in. He said to Hobbs, 'How's our vigilante hunter then?'

So he's figured out what I'm looking for in the files, Hobbs thought. He was taken aback. 'Vigilantes?' he said. 'What about vigilantes? Maybe they've got the right idea.'

'Sure they do,' Sergeant Howard said. 'Everyone ought to take it up. But then where would we be? We'd be out of a job.'

When Sergeant Howard wasn't looking, Hobbs called the prison where Naylor had been on remand to find his address. He was told they thought he'd gone to live in Falmouth but when Hobbs rang the police station in Falmouth he was told they'd never heard of him. Then Hobbs called the six Naylors in the local telephone book. They were all related to one another but none of them was related to Terence Charles Naylor, or at least no one wanted to admit it. Then Hobbs did what he should have done in the first place. He looked at Naylor's file again. Naylor's mother's name was Mrs Smith. There was an address but she did not live there any more. It had been crossed out and marked Out of Date, but there was no replacement. There were five pages of Smiths in the Salthaven telephone directory and Mrs Elizabeth Smith was not one of them. She could have moved out of town. If Hobbs were Naylor's mother, he would have left the country. Hobbs scoured the file for clues, but, of course, Naylor had been found not guilty so there was no reason to keep tabs on him.

Hobbs noticed the name of Naylor's school, though. It had been mentioned because part of the defence had been that Naylor had a good education and upbringing and no reason, as far as a middle-class jury could conceive, for raping a working-class Northern student he was unlikely ever to have met.

The school was the sort of place, Hobbs thought, where the old boys might keep in touch. It might be worth a try. He had some vague idea that if he could find Naylor, he could stop whatever awful thing he was afraid would happen. Hobbs didn't want anything bad to happen to Clementine Illingworth.

The next day Hobbs wasn't on duty until late so he drove out to Naylor's old school. It was the summer holidays. But at last he found an elderly man reading on a terrace.

Hobbs showed his warrant card.

'Simmonds,' the old man said. 'Housemaster.'

He put down his book to give Hobbs his full attention. 'We've had a great number of criminals here. Are you writing a newspaper article about us?'

'I'm a detective,' Hobbs said, 'not a journalist.'

'Attempting to detect what?'

'This was rape,' Hobbs said, then he added quickly, 'Alleged rape.'

'Alleged rape?' the old man said, as if that was beneath an Old Millistonian. 'We have had many ravishers. Well into the nineteenth century Old Millistonians were great ravishers.'

'He probably hasn't done anything,' Hobbs said. 'I'm trying to locate him.'

'We had an Old Boy hanged for ravishing at Oxford in 1646. But I can't see Naylor rising to that level. I'm afraid he'd be a mute and inglorious ravisher.'

Until then Hobbs had not realized that the old teacher remembered Naylor. The old man said, 'I recall he ran away from home to return to school. Then I met the mother and it was obvious why.'

'Why?'

'The sort who uses her child as the reason for her own failure. She wouldn't have been able to stand it if he'd been a happy and successful schoolboy. She'd have no one to blame then for her own unhappiness. I heard she got married. Poor sod.'

21

Half-awake, Naylor rolled over in bed. His eyes refused to focus. He had a hangover. He couldn't remember a thing.

Happily he saw he was in his own room, not in jail. He took in the familiar shape of the wardrobe and the window. But daylight hurt his eyes. It wasn't Monday morning, it was still Sunday evening, not even dark yet.

He turned his head. At first he thought the mattress had split. Wiry black stuff lay on the pillow beside him. Then he realized it was a woman's dark hair. He could make out a face on the pillow. At first he did not know who she was. Then details of what happened began to come back. It was Mary, Bert's daughter from the café. He had picked her up in the morning and he had been with her all day. He couldn't remember bringing her back home.

He tried to look at his watch, but he couldn't focus on the numbers on the face. He'd been drinking at work last night. The day staff had had some kind of party. He'd found a leftover bottle of whisky, half-full, in one of the empty offices. He didn't usually drink on the job, but he didn't usually find free whisky. Then early in the morning, after work, he'd made his way to Bert's Café as usual. It was closed. He'd peered through the window and saw Mary cleaning the tables.

She came across and unlocked the door to let him in.

'We're closed today,' she said.

'I got drunk,' he said. 'I'm mixed up. What day is it?'

He couldn't remember bringing her home. His mother wasn't in. She was still at church, singing and praying. He bragged to Mary about his mother being an interior designer. He enjoyed seeing that Mary was impressed by the bijou cottage stuffed with antiques. Upstairs she looked around his room, poking into his private life. She picked up one of his martial arts magazines.

'Never mind about that now,' he said coming up behind her and putting his hands on her tits.

He'd wished he hadn't brought her here. It was boring, and he didn't really fancy her; she was too eager. What he liked was when they fought him off, when they didn't want it. He supposed he'd passed out then.

Now the grandfather clock in the hall downstairs struck seven. He couldn't believe it. He would have to hurry.

He eased himself out of bed. The last thing he wanted was for Mary to wake up and talk to him. He picked his clothes off the floor, dressed, and went downstairs. He was angry with himself. Getting drunk like that could have spoiled everything when he'd been so careful tracking Tizzy down last week and eavesdropping on her making plans for tonight with the man Barry Pearson said was a big millionaire politician. He'd got her where he wanted her, the world would know the kind of woman she was. And he'd almost blown it.

Naylor guessed nothing was going to happen on the boat until later in the evening. If they weren't away by 8.30, they'd miss the tide until early morning, so he thought they were unlikely actually to be sailing. It was too early. There might still be people around who might recognize the famous man. The summer visitors didn't stay over a Sunday night. The place would be deserted after about nine. But he wanted to be on hand before that to be sure.

He was leaving the house when his mother came in.

'I've been to Evensong,' she said. 'I wish you'd come with me. You'd enjoy it. I know you would. You've got a lovely singing voice.'

'There's a naked whore upstairs in my

bed,' he said. 'You tell her about Evensong when she comes down.'

He slammed the front door on her moaning voice. Then he stood waiting for a bus into town. The service at weekends was hopeless. Finally he started to walk. When he was halfway to the next stop, a bus passed him. He tried to wave it down. The driver ignored him. The bastard enjoyed it, Naylor could see that. It made the little prick feel good. Naylor felt it was a bad omen.

Then he had a stroke of luck. A taxi slowed down as it passed him. Naylor caught the driver's eye and put out his hand and it stopped.

At the harbour there were crowds of people. They had come to enjoy themselves but there was nothing to do. Naylor went into a bar on the quayside and ordered a sandwich. Then he went to telephone Barry Pearson. I'm doing it right this time, Naylor said to himself. This time I'm doing everything right.

After that he couldn't sit still to eat the sandwich he'd ordered. He had to get up and be moving.

He left the bar and set out to walk to the marina. He moved like a blind man, ploughing through the crowds. People stepped to one side as they saw him coming towards them.

He did not take the main road along the cliff top, but cut across a narrow track along the rocks above the shoreline. The tide was coming in. The water lapped at his feet where the path ran close to the sea. A great cloud of screeching gulls, like white sheets of paper blowing in the wind, swirled round and round over something floating in the water. They were filthy scavengers. Naylor hated the noise they made.

The clock on the big church in the town centre struck. The sound ebbed and flowed in a breeze that kept changing direction. He lost count of the strokes. He hated all churches, even the ones his mother didn't go to. She had started going to church since her husband Mr Smith died. Mr Smith had had a heart condition. He was pretty old anyway. He'd tried to give Naylor a hard time, telling him not to talk that way to his mother. Naylor showed him. He started talking that way to him too. 'You knew he had a bad heart,' his mother had said. 'I forgot about it, OK?' Naylor shouted at her. Naylor didn't go to the funeral. His mother didn't get any more men after that. She was too old now for anyone to want to touch her. Naylor decided that she'd started all that religion stuff because God was the only person who could possibly think there was any point in her being alive at all any more. She was no use to Naylor: she wasn't going to find a man to leave her a lot of money now. Mr Smith hadn't left enough to cover his own funeral. It's just as well I can look after myself, Naylor thought. Barry Pearson would pay well.

Naylor was careful approaching the marina. He didn't want to be seen. The dying sun threw long, dense shadows across the car park. He kept close to the fence. If he kept in the shade he was invisible to anyone facing the sun.

He heard footsteps. He thought they were a man's, walking slowly. He pressed himself against the wall. He saw the big woman, the one who had almost caught him in her house. She was walking from the waterside towards her car. He recognized the car. Her head was bent, and she was dragging her feet, not looking at anything in particular. He thought she looked lopsided. He stood quite still, watching. She got in her car and drove away.

There was no one else about. The weekend sailors had all gone back to London. There was no one to see him walking slowly down the central pontoon towards the *Eumenides*. When he got close he could see the sexy little dark-haired bitch busy in the cockpit, cleaning up. He thought, I could take her now and she wouldn't be able to say a word about it. She wouldn't dare go to the cops about it. As for the old biddy, he'd think of something for her. He always wanted to give those old grannies a few good hard punches when he was forced to stand next to one of them in a shop or taking up space in a bus queue. They were so feeble. He liked to think of them folding up and crumbling into nothing if he hit them just one punch. It was their fault, the way they looked so helpless.

But he had to stop day-dreaming and concentrate on the boat. He wondered how much the little bitch had told the big one about what she was planning that night. She had evidently got rid of her anyway. Naylor could see that. The devious little Tizzy must have told her to keep away, which would account for the way the old girl looked when he saw her drive off. The little bitch couldn't have the old bag hanging about when she was fucking the big fish TV millionaire.

Naylor jumped down on to the *Topsy*'s sloping foredeck. It was slippery. He almost lost his footing. He cursed whoever owned the boat. It was a disgrace, the way they left her; they didn't deserve to have a boat. He sat on the little boat's deck and watched.

Naylor did not have long to wait. It was still light enough to see when the man came along the pontoon. He looked young. He looked much too young to be the big shot millionaire Barry Pearson said he was. It made Naylor cross to think of a young prick like this being a big shot who told the Prime Minister what to do. This time he wasn't wearing a suit, he had on jeans and some kind of jerkin. The man was a prat, but then the Prime Minister was a prat, too.

Naylor watched Wheeler climb over the boat's deckrail into the cockpit. He was carrying something, a bottle. She took it from him. Then they went below down the companionway.

Naylor waited. The last streaks of colour had faded from the sky and it was almost dark. He was about to climb back on to the pontoon to go to telephone Barry Pearson when he saw the little bitch reappear in the cockpit. She was silhouetted against the light from the open hatch.

'You stay there,' he heard her call back down the companionway. 'I'll just get the decks cleared and then we'll start.'

The man's voice came from the cabin. 'Anything I can do?'

She laughed. 'You? No, you stay where you are. It's going to be a glorious night.'

She was taking the boat out. It had never occurred to him that she would take her prize catch out of the marina for a sail. It complicated things. Naylor moved along the pontoon as quickly as he could without making any noise.

When he got on the phone he told Pearson, 'She's taking him out in the boat.'

'Well, that's that,' the journalist said. 'We can't stow away.' There was music playing in the background. Naylor could hear a woman singing along to it.

'Leave it to me,' Naylor said. 'You just get your arse down here. We'll follow them.'

But when he put the phone down, he'd no idea what to do. He had to get his hands on a boat. They had to catch up with the yacht and then be able to get away afterwards.

There were several small motor boats tied up alongside the pontoon. He wondered if it was possible to get one going with the electric leads, like a car. He didn't know how to do it. Pearson might know, but it was too dangerous to take a chance on Pearson having the knack. Also Pearson might not want to steal a boat.

Naylor looked across the marina basin. There was a light inside the nightwatchman's hut. That's where the weekenders would leave their spare keys.

Old Ted was not there. The door was locked. When Naylor peered through the filthy window, he could see the panel of keyhooks on the wall. He checked the lock on the door. It was old. The door jamb was crumbling. Naylor stood back and kicked the lock. He could feel the jamb shift. Two more kicks and the wood gave way.

There was a printed number above each hook. The keys were tagged. That was no use to him. He did not know the berth numbers of the motor boats. He ignored multiple sets of keys. The kind of boat he was looking for had no cabin to lock. What he wanted was an ignition key and nothing else. He was in a sweat. He could imagine the dark-haired little whore's boat slipping out to sea where he'd never be able to find her.

He took all the suitable keys he could see. Then he left the hut, shutting the door as best he could behind him. If the old nightwatchman was drunk enough, he might not notice the lock had been broken before morning.

Barry Pearson was already coming towards him across the tarmac outside the shuttered mall. He had two cameras slung around his neck.

'Hey,' Pearson said, 'have they gone?'

Naylor pointed to the mast light of a boat making for the channel.

'That's her,' he said.

Naylor crossed from one boat to another trying the keys in the ignitions.

'What are you doing? Don't you have a boat?'

'I'm borrowing one.'

'Christ,' the journalist said. Then he laughed. 'I don't know anything about this,' he said. 'If anyone asks me, I say I thought it was your boat. You told me it was your boat.'

Naylor found a key that fitted. 'Quick,' he said, 'cast off.'

The engine fired twice and died. Across the water Naylor could hear the throttle note from the *Eumenides* change as she reached clear water. He checked the gauges on the speed boat, the fuel tank was full. He pulled out the choke. There was a loud gurgle and a gust of fumes exploded into the water through the stern gland. The engine started.

'Now, you little bitch,' Naylor said.

'What's that?'

'Nothing,' Naylor said. 'Just talking to myself.'

The moon went behind a cloud and it was pitch dark now. Naylor manoeuvred the boat away from the pontoon and out into the open water.

'Where is she?' Pearson said. They couldn't see the boat. 'We've lost her,' he said, 'we might as well turn back.'

Then the moon sailed out from behind the cloud.

'There she is,' Naylor said.

He pointed ahead along the broad ivory trail where the reflecting moon cast a pale beam across the dark water. They could see the shadow of the yacht as she moved slowly ahead of them, the light at her masthead like a star. Naylor throttled back so as not to get too close.

22

Fiona steered a course up the centre of the channel towards the open sea. The tide was running with them. In the moonlight streaks of spilled fuel on the water glowed with dark opal iridescence. She thought of Clem hidden in the sail-locker under the foredeck and she was glad it was Clem and not her down there in the dark.

Bruce Wheeler came up the companionway into the cockpit. 'What a marvellous moon,' he said. 'My God, it's beautiful. I thought it would just be dark.'

She made an effort at conversation. 'Where are you from?' Fiona said. 'Aren't you from here?'

'London,' he said. 'Only from London. I come down here from time to time when Dad makes his royal visits to the country house. What about you? Where are you from?'

'Oh,' she said, 'all over the place.' It wasn't something she liked talking about. Bruce Wheeler didn't pursue the subject. Fiona was under no illusion that this was out of sensitivity, but because he wasn't interested.

'The sky's so huge,' Wheeler said. 'Look at

those stars. In London you can scarcely see the stars.' He sounded like a boy on a first sea trip.

'I love going out at night,' she said. 'It's quiet and secret.' She thought he might put his arm about her but he didn't. She wished again that the two of them were off for a perfectly ordinary sail; that he had never called her a hick little secretary, and rejected her when she wanted to make love; that they could simply enjoy a good night out together on the boat. But he had to pay.

Somewhere close to shore they could hear the low throb of another engine, much more powerful than theirs.

'What's that?' he asked.

'Fishermen, probably,' Fiona said. 'Checking lobster pots. They catch all sorts of shellfish round Studholme.'

'It's a different world,' he said. 'And you really belong in it. You surprise me. You've got hidden depths.'

She thought he would get romantic now but he didn't.

He was leaning against the side of the cockpit staring at the water. 'This is wonderful,' he said. 'Perhaps I should get a boat. Maybe you could teach me how to handle it.'

The motion of the boat changed as they

reached the open sea. The wind had dropped but the water was still choppy. Studholme Island loomed on the starboard bow. The engine beat deepened and quickened as Fiona moved the accelerator handle at the back of the engine casing with her foot.

'You'd better go below,' she said.

'Can't I help?' he asked.

She made an effort to keep a note of contempt out of her voice. Any fool could see he was not the stuff of a real sailor. It made her feel good to be condescending. 'No,' she said. 'You don't know where anything is. If it gets rougher, you'll be in the way.'

The sea was much heavier now. He swayed, trying to keep his feet. He laughed. 'Look at me,' he said, 'falling all over the place, and I wanted to kiss you. I guess I'll have to wait till later. I'd probably stumble and take your eye out.'

He was being nice, but however nice he was, she wasn't going to relent. 'Don't worry,' she said, 'I'm not going anywhere. We'll come inshore again soon, once we're round the island. It'll be calmer there.'

Bruce Wheeler left the cockpit and she heard him stumble against the navigation table on his way to the cabin. He turned on the radio. She recognized an aria from *Tosca*. God, she thought, it may be a cliché, but it's so damned romantic. She identified with *Tosca*.

When they reached the cove the sea bed fell steeply away at the foot of the cliffs. She knew it was safe enough to bring the yacht in close to the shingle beach to anchor. Once under the cliffs, the boat would be invisible from the land except for the beach where Marjorie would be waiting. Then once she was on board whatever was going to happen would happen.

She was coming in towards the island cove too fast. She cut the engine and brought the bow into the wind. She dropped the tiller and moved quickly forward to release the anchor. The chain rattled out. She could still hear the powerful engine of the other boat, and she wondered what they were doing. They seemed to be going to fish in the wrong place. Tourists, she thought. On the radio Tosca was still singing. The cliffs had a stereophonic effect. Fiona could feel tears in her eyes, it was so beautiful. She knelt on the foredeck to raise the hatch cover over the sail locker.

'You OK?' she whispered.

Clem's pale face appeared in the opening. She nodded. 'Give me a hand,' she said. Fiona reached down and pulled her out.

Clem crouched on the deck beside Fiona. She closed the hatch cover behind her. 'I'll put the ladder down over the stern for Marjorie,' Clem said, keeping her voice low.

Fiona made as much noise as possible to cover Clem moving about the deck. Then she went below.

Clem heard her greet the man. She heard her say, 'I need a drink.' The music stopped. The man said something Clem couldn't hear.

Clem looked across the stretch of black water to the shore. It was very dark. It was a clear night but the cliffs blocked the moonlight. She thought of Marjorie waiting on the mainland, peering across the water for sight or sound of the boat. Clem didn't envy Marjorie finding her way through the rocks down the narrow, steep path to the beach, carrying the deflated rubber dinghy and the foot pump. But she'd have had plenty of daylight left when she did it. And Marjorie was physically strong from working out at the gym, even if she hadn't managed to lose much weight. It was inside that Marjorie was weak. The same as me, Clem said to herself, I'm weak inside. I can't even go home to face my own mother.

Clem strained to hear Marjorie rowing the rubber dinghy, but the noise of a boat engine further out to sea swamped any other sound. She peered into the dark to catch a glimpse of the rubber dinghy approaching. Close by she heard the shrill whine of a powerful motorboat engine being revved. Then she remembered. She'd forgotten the signal. Marjorie would be waiting for her to flash the light and Clem had left the torch in the sail locker.

Moving as quietly as she could, she went back to the hatch cover. She lifted it and stretched forward to fold it back gently against the foot of the mast. The boat suddenly lurched. The motor boat was closer than she thought, its wake made the yacht rear up. Unbalanced, she pitched forward, hitting her head against the mast footing. The hatch cover banged back as she slumped unconscious in the narrow gap between the side of the cabin and the deck rail.

In the cabin Wheeler raised his head. 'What was that?' he asked.

'Gust of wind,' Fiona said. Why did he have to be so nervous? Damn Marjorie, she thought, that must have been her heaving herself on board. But at least she was on board. Now they could get on with what they had come to do. But Bruce was slow. He was one of those men who made you make the moves, but he looked surprised when she took off her clothes.

'What's wrong?' she said seeing him just sitting there. 'Oh, Christ, you don't like me?

Listen, I'm terribly sorry.' She started to put her blouse back on and was buttoning it up, looking about for where she had thrown her jeans. But he put his arms round her. He wanted her now, she could see that. She pushed him away.

'What's the matter?' he said.

She looked at him sitting there on the berth where she had shoved him. He had that subnormal look they sometimes had when they were getting carried away.

'I can't,' she said. 'I'm sorry. I wanted to. I thought I did. But not like this. Not if you don't —'

He came for her then. He put his arm round her, holding her against him as he unzipped his jeans and pushed them down below his knees.

She tried to push him away again but she couldn't shift him. 'Let's go sailing,' she said, 'and maybe later.'

'What's this?' he said. 'What's the matter? You're the one who took your clothes off.'

She stood up, reaching for her jeans. He caught her arms and pushed her down against the berth.

'I don't want to,' she said.

'Just relax,' he said, 'it'll be all right.' He was holding her arms, his body pressing her down on the bunk. She felt him enter her.

'You're hurting me,' she said. 'This is rape.'

'It's nice,' he said. 'Oh, my God! It's wonderful, you're beautiful.'

There was a loud noise in the companionway. Gasping, he raised his head. There was another crash outside the cabin.

'What the hell's going on?' he asked.

Over Bruce Wheeler's shoulder, Fiona saw a man standing inside the cabin.

There was a flash of light. Wheeler tried to turn and get to his feet. The man took another picture before running up the companionway, and then she could hear him running on the deck.

A powerful engine revved alongside the yacht's hull, a monstrous sudden sound. Then it was gone.

'What happened? What was that?' she asked.

Bruce Wheeler hit her hard in the face.

'You bloody little bitch,' he said.

23

By the look of the painfully blue sky through the yellow-curtained window the morning was well on. Clem was confused. There was something she knew she had to do but her head hurt and she couldn't think. When she tried to get up the room tipped, adding to the surreal effect. Am I ill? she thought. She put a hand to her head and felt the swelling above her left eye. Then she remembered Fiona telling her something over and over again but she did not know what it was she'd been telling her. It was like trying to remember the details of a dream.

Very carefully she got to her feet. The room started to spin, then gradually slowed and stopped. She was stiff, her whole body ached, her left shoulder was painful when she moved it, and all the colours in the room, and the sky outside, the blue sky outside the window with the yellow curtains, were much too bright.

She tried to think. Something had happened on the boat. She remembered waking up on the deck of the boat, back in the marina, with Fiona shaking her and then bringing her back here in her car. There'd been something wrong with Fiona's face. She didn't seem to be able to speak properly. Clem couldn't remember how she'd got to bed. Marjorie hadn't been there.

Then she heard Marjorie's voice shouting out from downstairs, 'Clem! Clem, come quickly.'

Clem had to take deep breaths before she could move. She went to the top of the stairs, stiff-legged, clutching the banister, and came down slowly as if the stairs might suddenly give way.

'What is it?' she said. She could scarcely hold her head up. The light in the room was terribly bright and the television was too loud.

Marjorie was standing on the hearthrug pointing at the television. 'Look at that,' she said.

Clem looked at the screen. A newscaster was saying something about the famous Tom Wheeler, speaking about him as though he'd just died. Then Bruce Wheeler's face appeared on the screen.

'Not him,' Marjorie said. 'There was a picture of Fiona.'

It made no more sense to Clem than if Marjorie had said that she had seen Fiona riding a surfboard in the street outside.

'Is he dead?' Clem asked. She thought now that it must be Bruce Wheeler who was dead. But he couldn't be. They had been on the boat last night. Bruce Wheeler had been on the boat. Something had happened. All their plans had gone wrong.

The screen showed a photograph of Bruce Wheeler with a woman with naked breasts. He was practically naked himself. His face was turned to the camera, frozen in a blurred expression of horror.

'So,' she said, 'Fiona was right about him.'

'No, no, didn't you see?' Marjorie said. 'That was Fiona!'

'Fiona?'

Clem looked back at the television. The newscaster had moved on to another story. Marjorie turned the set off. She sat down heavily on the settee. Then for the first time she saw the bruise on Clem's head. 'My God,' she said, 'what happened to you? Did he do that?'

'I don't know,' Clem said. 'Don't you know? I think I'm concussed.'

Marjorie didn't know what to say. The image of Wheeler bent over Fiona filled her mind.

'I didn't give you the signal,' Clem said. 'I remember now. I was going back to get the torch.'

For a moment Marjorie was tempted to let Clem blame herself. Then she said, 'Clem, I didn't go to the cove. One of my migraines came on and I took the pills and went to lie down, and I didn't wake up. But who took the picture? Where did they get that picture?'

Clem shook her head. She was shivering. They were silent for a while. Then Marjorie started towards the kitchen. 'I'll make coffee,' she said. 'Or would you rather have tea? You'd better have tea.'

When Marjorie came in with the tea, Clem asked, 'What did they say? About the picture?'

'It was published in one of the tabloids this morning.'

'How? How did they get it? There was no one else on the boat.'

'You think she set up a camera and then sold the picture?'

'Marjorie, that's ridiculous. That picture isn't going to do Fiona any good at all.'

'I just thought . . . for the money.'

'That's horrible. She wouldn't risk everything she's got like that. How can you think such a thing?'

'I don't,' Marjorie said. 'I just can't think how else anyone got a picture like that. Do you think she's at work? Maybe she doesn't know about it. She wouldn't read that sort of paper.'

'Oh, my God,' Clem said, 'she'll know by now if she's gone to work.'

'I'm going to ring her,' Marjorie said. 'We've got to know if she's all right.'

'I feel terrible,' Clem said. 'If I hadn't fallen — '

'It's my fault,' Marjorie said. 'If I'd been there . . .'

Marjorie tried to ring Fiona's mobile phone but the number was switched off. When she rang Fiona's work number a woman said, 'I'm sorry, she's in a meeting.'

'When will she be out?'

'I'm sorry I have no information.'

Marjorie put the phone down. Then she became concerned about Clem's head. 'You've got to have that looked at.'

'It's all right,' Clem said, but Marjorie insisted on driving her to the casualty department at the hospital where Clem was told she was suffering from concussion. They told her to rest. Marjorie said she'd take her home and see that she stayed in bed.

Clem was sleeping when the lunchtime news came on the TV. Fiona's face filled the screen. Her face was bruised, one cheek was swollen and her lip had been cut. She spoke in a throaty little whisper as if someone had been throttling her.

Fiona was accusing Bruce Wheeler, son of the media mogul, the Prime Minister's special adviser on industry, of rape. Bruce Wheeler, it seemed, was consulting his solicitor. Then there were pictures of Tom Wheeler outside the Home Office, and Bruce Wheeler at the centre of a mass of men and women with notebooks, cameras and microphones. His blond head shone like a beacon as he made his way through them.

Marjorie turned off the television. She sat and looked at the blank screen.

24

Fiona had put on make-up to hide the bruising where Bruce Wheeler had struck her, but under the harsh light in the office cloakroom it didn't look too well hidden.

Frank Borden was waiting to see her as soon as she came in. She would never forget his face. He didn't even ask what had happened. She had never seen him so stern, at least with her. The board had already held a meeting about it, Frank said, and they were unanimous.

Then Frank Borden dropped his stern look and became quite fatherly. It wasn't his decision, he said. He wanted to keep her. He liked her. She'd always done a good job. But she must see the company couldn't employ her to represent it with the public. Not any more. He'd suggested finding her something else in the firm, but the other board members said keeping her on would be bad for business.

That was when she said Bruce Wheeler had raped her.

She saw the shock on Frank Borden's face. She wiped off her make-up to show her bruises. She could see that it was very shocking to Frank Borden.

'He'll say you agreed,' he said. 'Why else would you go sailing alone with him and be anchored in a quiet cove at night? That's what he'll say.'

'I wasn't alone,' Fiona said. 'My friend Clem was on the boat.'

'Clem?' She could see he thought this was a man.

'Clementine. My friend Clementine Illingworth. She came with us.'

'What happened to her?'

'She was knocked out.'

'How?'

'I don't know. I was down below.'

'Are you saying Bruce Wheeler knocked her out?'

'I don't know. I said I was down below. He certainly hit me.'

Frank Borden stood up and came round to her side of the desk and patted her shoulder. Then he went out to see the other members of the board and Fiona went into his bathroom and made sure all the make-up was washed off. When he came back he said she was not being given the sack, that there was a principle involved and they were all behind her.

'That face looks nasty,' he said, 'you'd

better have it seen to. Or perhaps the police doctor will need to see it.' He saw that she didn't understand, and his protective instincts were aroused. 'My poor girl,' he said. 'I've called the police. You can't let him get away with this. They'll need evidence. All the evidence they can get. This isn't going to be easy for you. Wheeler will buy the best lawyers in the land.'

Fiona stood and smiled although it hurt her lip. Frank Borden was very old-fashioned. He offered her his arm and held the door for her.

'Don't worry,' he said, 'we're going to fight that brute.'

'You're a real friend, Frank. You know I wouldn't let you down. But we don't want the media circus here, do we? I'll take the heat off by staying away for a few days. But now I'd better go and see if my poor friend Clem's all right. Then I'll go down to the police station.'

Fiona left Frank Borden's office. As she waited for the lift, she heard her name called. She turned to see Tim Yates hurrying towards her. He grabbed her arm.

'Tim?' Fiona asked. It was a question because she thought she'd made a mistake. He looked like a different person. He looked scruffy and ill.

'It's all right,' he said, 'everything's going to

be all right.' He was trying to catch his breath.

She could feel his hand on her arm trembling as though he had fever.

He pushed into the lift with her and the automatic door closed. 'I've told my wife,' he said.

'Told your wife what?' Fiona said.

'About us.'

He seemed to be trying to embrace her. She pushed him away. 'Us?' she said. 'What about us?'

'I told her I'm in love with you and I want us to be together. I'll look after you now.'

'Stop it,' she said. 'You're talking rubbish. There's no *us*.'

'But I've told her. She's thrown me out. We can be together.'

The lift came to a stop and the door opened. Fiona stepped out. 'There's no *us*,' she said again. 'There never will be. You're pathetic.'

She walked away from him without looking back.

She drove away through a small band of reporters already gathered at the entrance gates. They ran to their cars to follow as she drove to Marjorie's house.

When Marjorie answered the door, she stared at Fiona and Fiona could see that she was scared.

'How did you get here?' Marjorie said.

She didn't ask Fiona in, but she didn't stop her when Fiona pushed past her and walked into the hall.

'Where's Clem?' Fiona said. 'She should hear this, and I'm having trouble talking.'

Clem had heard Fiona arrive and she came downstairs.

'I'm feeling much better,' Clem said, pre-empting Marjorie's fussing. She looks like a ghost, Marjorie thought.

Fiona was being business-like. She talked as if she were ticking items off a shopping list when she told Marjorie and Clem her story of the rape. In spite of her swollen face, she was so bright it was incredible.

'Look,' Fiona said, 'I've got an idea. We all need time. I've got leave of absence and you could get away, Clem, and there's nothing to stop Marjorie. Let's take a trip in the boat. Just a few days, but we can get away from the cops' questions and the Press and everything till things cool down. It'll give us a chance to sort ourselves out.'

'You can't go,' Marjorie said. 'You can't accuse someone of rape and then take a holiday. The police will want to talk to you.'

'Well, of course I won't tell them I'm going,' Fiona said. 'Let them find out I've gone after we've left. They can't stop me.'

'You can't go through with this,' Marjorie said. 'I don't believe a word of it.'

'A word of what?' Fiona asked. 'You don't believe I was raped? I was. I told him no, but he didn't stop.'

'What sort of position was he in when you finally told him to stop?'

'Christ, Marjorie,' Fiona said, 'you sound like some man. It's rape once I said no. I said no but he didn't stop. He hit me. Where do you think I got this face? I couldn't even struggle with him. He hit me and just shoved it in.'

Marjorie blinked hearing that expression. 'Well,' she said, 'I don't know. He must have been carried away. You must've let it go too far.'

'Carried away?' Fiona said with great sarcasm. 'They all say that. The man who raped your Tessa would say he was carried away. If a woman says no, she means no, and if a man doesn't stop it's rape. That's the law. For Christ's sake, I told the cops and they believe me.'

'What about evidence?' Marjorie asked.

'They've taken samples and they've seen the bruises.'

'You took him there for him to have sex with you,' Marjorie said. 'Did you tell the police that?'

'Well, I'm going sailing,' Fiona said. 'It's obvious you don't want to come.'

'I'll come.' Clem said. 'It's a good idea if we get away for a few days.'

'I tell you, I'm not coming,' Marjorie said. She stood up, scraping her chair back. 'And I'll tell you another thing, Fiona. If you go ahead with this charge against Bruce Wheeler, I'll be the one going to the police. I'll tell them everything.'

'You wouldn't dare,' Fiona said.

'Drop those charges or you'll find out,' Marjorie said.

'Come on,' Clem said. 'Don't let's fight among ourselves.'

Fiona got up to go. 'Oh, yes, Clem,' she said, 'how do you feel? I should've taken you to the hospital last night. I'm taking you there now. You must have concussion at least. Look at that bump on your head.'

'She's been,' Marjorie said. 'I took her this morning.'

'That's good,' Fiona said. 'There has to be a record of her needing treatment. We must have everything on the record. Otherwise it's just our word against his.'

'Our word?' Marjorie said. 'Clem wasn't raped.'

'Well,' Fiona said, 'she was there. I told the police she was there.' Fiona turned to Clem.

'You got knocked out. You don't know what hit you, do you?'

'My God, Fiona,' Marjorie said, 'you can't drag Clem into this.'

'She's already in. She was there.'

Marjorie took Fiona by the shoulders and shook her. She was disconcerted at how small and bony Fiona was. She pushed the girl away, feeling like some huge hawk about to rip a small bird to pieces. But she couldn't stay silent.

'I mean it, Fiona. You drop the charges against Bruce Wheeler or I go to the police and confess the lot.'

Fiona shrugged. 'You won't,' she said. 'You've too much to lose.'

'No, I've very little to lose. Unlike you. You're enjoying all this attention, aren't you? Well, I've warned you; it's your decision.'

Fiona went, not to sneak out the back way, but to the front door. Marjorie could see reporters gathered round outside and her neighbours watching from their doorways and front windows. Fiona opened the door, hesitated for a moment on the top step, and then walked out.

Marjorie watched Fiona hurry to her car. Fiona was holding a hand to her bruised face, but she was covering the side of her face that was unmarked.

25

Naylor touched the breast pocket of his uniform jacket to make sure Barry Pearson's money was still there. It was more than he'd ever had in his hand all at the same time. That was good, but soon he'd have more, much more. The women would pay him plenty to keep his mouth shut. And they'd keep on paying.

He walked towards Bert's Café seeing himself strolling among palm trees in the sun in a really good foreign place.

'You look pleased with yourself,' Mary said when he threw open the door of the café and marched in like the true adventurer he was. But he avoided her eyes.

The place was crowded, but no one looked up when he came in. He knew what that meant. He should probably teach her a lesson; but then he didn't care, let them think what they liked. He'd soon be leaving all this behind him. Anyone who stood in his way now would be punished. He had proved he could do it. Barry Pearson hadn't been best pleased when he found that it wasn't the big noise father on the boat, but only the playboy son. But he'd got such a good picture he hadn't minded too much. The sins of the children are visited on the father, he said, and he'd handed over the money.

Bert's customers were laughing and shouting at one another. Naylor saw the obscene gestures they were making.

'What's up? What are they on about?' he asked the man seated at the table next to his.

'Tom Wheeler's resignation,' the man said. He showed Naylor the local paper. 'You can bet on it, he's been fired,' the man said. 'The PM's a big family man. He couldn't have an adviser with a son like that.'

Naylor didn't bother reading the story. He felt elated. I did that, he told himself. He had secret power. Of course, he'd always known that, but other people hadn't believed him. Naylor laughed. The men all around him were laughing. Naylor joined in their laughter. For the first time he felt at one with the men in Bert's Café. He roared along with them when they made crude jokes about Tom Wheeler's arrogant prick of a son caught out with the local tart.

But then Mary came from the kitchen and started screaming at them. 'You're all animals,' she shouted at the men. 'You're disgusting. What he did to that girl.'

'She was asking for it,' one man said. 'She

211

got what she was looking for.'

Mary banged Naylor's plate down on the table. She had her head turned, addressing the room. 'What do you mean? What chance did she have? Can't a girl expect a man like that to be a gentleman?'

'Aw, pull the other one, love,' a driver with a cockney accent said scornfully. 'Hot little number like that? If you ask me, she was begging for it.'

Mary had her hands on her hips. 'You stupid bastards,' she screamed at them. They started to laugh. They waited for her to scream at them some more. 'Oh,' she said, 'you're all so fucking stupid! That girl's not like the girls you know, the slags who go with you. She wasn't looking for it. They were taking him for a trip on the boat. She wasn't alone. She had her girlfriend there.'

'What?' Naylor said. 'What friend? What friend was there?'

Mary turned and looked at him. 'There was another girl on the boat. But she got knocked out. That man knocked her friend out and then he raped her. If you ask me, she's brave going to the cops. She's bloody brave telling on the Prime Minister's best friend's son. She's a heroine. Every woman will think so. She's a bloody heroine.'

Naylor read the newspaper headline now.

212

'Second Girl On Sex Sail', he read. He hadn't seen a second girl. The little tart's made it up, he thought. She's got one of her friends to say she was there to support the rape story. As if you had to rape a tart like that. My God, he thought, what a fucking little bitch. And she's going to get away with it. That vicious bitch would be a heroine, Mary said so. Mary was saying it again, screaming at the men to shut their mouths. The men were silent. Then they said that Mary was probably right. They agreed with her. The woman on the boat was a heroine going to the police to tell on a powerful man like Tom Wheeler's son. They could see that now. Naylor's plans had gone wrong. He didn't understand it. The power over things that he'd felt within him hadn't really been there. He'd been fooling himself again.

He had to get out of the steamy café. He got to his feet.

'What's wrong with you?' Mary said. 'I want to talk to you. I liked your mother. She told me about it. I know a boy like you wouldn't do a thing like that, what they said you did. I should know.'

Naylor looked at her and then looked away. He felt sick. His own mother had told this complete stranger about him. He brushed Mary aside.

'Hey,' she shouted at him, 'what's wrong with you now?'

But he did not look back. He set off along the Dock Road towards the marina. He did not know what he would do when he got there but he felt he needed to make contact with that little bitch again.

He found the marina car park full of vehicles and crowds of people. There were two television vans trailing black cable. The link chain gates between the car park and the mall were closed. Behind them, scowling like an angry old ape, Ted, the nightwatchman, watched the milling people. 'You're trespassing,' he was shouting at them. You're all trespassers.' They ignored him.

Naylor pushed his way through to the gate. His security guard uniform gave him authority. People made way for him. He was strong again. He was full of purpose once more.

'Hello, Ted,' Naylor said. 'Remember me?'

The old man stared at him. 'You're not with these buggers, are you?'

Naylor looked over his shoulder at the throng. 'Not me,' he said. 'Who are they?'

'Press, they call themselves. Bloody hooligans.'

'Need a hand?' Naylor said. 'Another of us in uniform could be a help.'

Ted took a while to think this over. Then he unlocked the gate and opened it just enough for Naylor to slip through. Naylor held it shut as Ted relocked it. The reporters pressed forward. 'Bugger off,' Ted told them.

Naylor shouted, 'You won't be allowed through these gates. The police have been called. Anyone attempting to break in will be arrested. Do you understand?'

For a moment his voice made them stop. But one reporter came up to the fence close to Naylor.

'Listen,' he said, 'you look as though you know how it is. Can't you tell us anything about Fiona Farr? There could be money in it.'

'Money?' Old Ted said. 'What money?'

'Fiona Farr?' Naylor said. 'Who's Fiona Farr?'

The reporter laughed. 'Where've you been, mate?' he said. 'The bint with Tom Wheeler's son.'

'That's not her name,' Naylor said. 'I know her name.'

Old Ted had wedged himself between Naylor and the reporter. His eyes had lit up at the prospect of money. Naylor was going to push him aside but there were too many people watching.

'Of course it's her name,' the reporter said.

'What do you think we're doing here?'

'She's got a Greek name,' Naylor said. 'Tizzy something.'

The reporter didn't say anything, he merely looked at Naylor as though he was someone retarded who had been given a uniform and a token job.

Naylor saw the way the reporter looked at him and he felt weak and stupid again. She had been fooling him. Tizzy, short for something Greek, had been just another lie.

Old Ted said to the reporter, 'I'll be in the pub later.' Then he walked to his hut. Naylor followed him.

'They don't know,' Old Ted said, 'but I do. She'll be here tonight. She's taking the boat out tonight.'

There was a bottle of rum in the hut. He offered the bottle to Naylor, who only pretended to drink from it.

The old man said, 'She's running out on all this. A few days to get away.' The old man looked around and shrugged. 'I been up all night,' he said. 'Look, you're a good fellow. I'm going up to the pub for a drop of whisky. Look after this place for me. There'll be a good drink in it for you. She gave me something to keep my trap shut. I'll see you're all right.'

Naylor waited until Ted crossed the car

park. Then he went to the panel of keyhooks and took the keys for berth thirty-six.

Naylor went down the pontoon and climbed on board the yacht. He unlocked the cabin hatch and went below. There were unwashed glasses on the table. He tripped on a cushion on the floor. He kicked it. An old blue sleeping bag was crammed into the pilot berth. A dog-eared paperback lay on the navigation desk. There was the stale ingrained smell of human sleep in a confined space. It was a prison smell. Nothing ever killed that smell, Naylor thought, but he had only got it for a moment when he first came into the closed cabin. He sniffed for it again but it had gone.

He went through to the forward sail locker. Three canvas sacks like punchbags were stacked on the locker shelf. Those were the stowed sails. He unlocked the forehatch and left it on the latch in order to be able to open it from the deck. Then he went out the way he came, relocking the cabin. He took the keys back to Ted's hut and put them back where he had found them.

The hut was dark. The window was so smeared the light could not get in even in the daytime. Naylor put on the light. In the corner was a heap of blankets which he took to be Ted's bed. Naylor picked through the old man's junk until he found a seaman's sweater. It was dirty and worn but Naylor took off his uniform jacket, folding it carefully, and put on the seaman's sweater. It smelled like an old dying dog.

He sat on the edge of the table peering through the dirty glass of the window. No one would even care he was gone. Mary would think he hadn't shown up for breakfast because his mother had told her about him. His mother wouldn't think anything of him not coming home. She was used to it. After a week or so, she'd wonder where he'd gone, but she wouldn't worry, not for ages.

Naylor looked around the hut. There was a small axe hanging on the back of the door. He took it down and tested the blade. It would be easy to crack the old man's head open. But he didn't have to kill him. He went to replace the axe but decided to keep it, he thought it might come in useful for threatening Tizzy or whatever she called herself. She'd know he meant business if he showed it to her. Then she'd come across with the money. He thought it might be good to get her to sail him to France. He could have a good time then, fucking her whenever he felt the urge. He'd make her sit with him in a restaurant where the French would think he was a rich English gentleman with a

218

beautiful mistress. She'd stink of fear but only he would be able to smell it, and to him it would be like the most expensive perfume.

Naylor made his way along the pontoon. He walked slowly, as if he was enjoying the fresh air. The wind made the halyards rattle against the metal masts of the yachts. Naylor stood and took a deep breath. He watched a gull swoop to pick up something from the water. Beyond the marina entrance, a slow-moving dredger inched its way up the channel. Naylor had a long wait ahead of him but he was feeling good again, he was feeling powerful once more.

26

Hobbs heard in the afternoon that Fiona Farr had dropped the rape charge against Bruce Wheeler.

With a great air of resoluteness she had come, practically marching, into the police station and said that on reflection she couldn't go through with the publicity of a court case. Too many other people would suffer. And it might be hard to make a rape charge stick. She knew very well who they were dealing with, and also the kind of pressure that rich and influential people could bring to bear. Miss Farr knew the trouble other women had had when they made accusations of this kind, and because of the nature of the case she could not hide behind the anonymity of Miss X. She would be made, she said, to look an absolute tart.

Hobbs also heard a story that Bruce Wheeler was going to bring an action for slander against Miss Farr, but it was only a story. Tom Wheeler had been forced to resign, but Hobbs wasn't convinced that the son could argue damage from that. From what Hobbs had heard, Bruce Wheeler didn't have much of a reputation with women to defend.

Hobbs had read Fiona Farr's earlier statement about the rape on the boat and he hadn't believed a word of it. At the same time, he couldn't believe she had set up Bruce Wheeler. He thought he would probably never know the game she was playing. She was a mystery. But there was the question of Clementine Illingworth, and Fiona Farr's assertion that she had been on board the yacht that night. Hobbs was keen to know the truth of that. Of course he had no business investigating it. If Sergeant Howard discovered that he was still thinking about vigilantes he'd be angry. But Hobbs had seen the marks on Martin Bakewell's back, he'd heard the story of Terry Naylor's scars. There was something there all right. If it wasn't Fiona Farr, with Clementine Illingworth and Mrs Warren — and even thinking of Mrs Warren being involved made him feel ridiculous — then it could be some other vigilantes. The dogged Hobbs wanted to know.

He went to the Fitness Centre, but they told him Clem was taking a few days off. He went to Mrs Warren's house. She invited him into her drawing-room and before he even asked for Clementine Illingworth she said, 'You've missed Clem. She's gone out.'

'I didn't come to see Miss Illingworth,' Hobbs said. He took the photograph from his pocket. 'Do you know this man?' he asked.

He was sure she recognized Naylor but she said, 'Who is he?'

'Terence Charles Naylor,' Hobbs said.

'I've never heard of him,' Mrs Warren said and handed him back the picture. 'What's he done?' Then she hesitated. 'Was that . . . Clem?'

'He was tried for rape,' Hobbs said. 'I think he was the one who broke in here.'

'To rape *me*?' She laughed. 'He knew I was out, didn't he? That's what you said at the time.' She might have been speaking to a silly child.

Then she asked, 'Why do you think it was him?'

'Just some evidence that makes us believe it might be. I showed Naylor's photograph to Miss Illingworth. She recognized him.'

'Well, if that's Terence Naylor, she would, wouldn't she?' Mrs Warren said. Then she added, 'She never mentioned it to me.'

He could see she was nervous, in spite of her imperious manner. She suddenly sat down and then she got up again and stood looking out of the window.

She asked, 'Why did you show that picture to Clem?'

'I think there's a connection,' Hobbs said. 'I think there's something connecting you and Miss Illingworth and Miss Farr with Terence Naylor.'

'Miss Farr?' she said. 'I think Miss Farr has been connected enough. I think Miss Farr has had all the connection she can handle for now.' She still had her back to him, looking out of the window as if it were the most casual of conversations. Then she asked, 'What connection could there be?'

'I think you know what it is, Mrs Warren. You know what connection.'

'Do you mean this man may have murdered my daughter?'

That thought hadn't occurred to him. He cursed himself for giving her the opportunity to make him feel brutal. He didn't know what to say.

She must have sensed his hesitation. She turned from the window.

'I'm sorry,' she said. 'I can't help you.' Her voice was steely, the same as when she said 'I think that Miss Farr has been connected enough'.

She was looking straight at him now. Hobbs turned away. 'I'll see myself out,' he said.

He would get no further with her that day. He had thought he'd got a chance, until she thought of Naylor in connection with her daughter's disappearance. There was nothing at all to connect Naylor with the Tessa Warren case, but she had jumped to that conclusion anyway. She must suspect everyone, he thought. Then he corrected himself: every man.

Hobbs went back to the station. He was sitting doing his expenses when the telephone rang.

'Inspector Hobbs,' an old man's voice said, 'this is Simmonds from Milliston College. You were seeking the whereabouts of one of our Old Boys. I've found his new address. His mother wrote from there to the school when he settled down here. She didn't want him to miss our school mag.'

Hobbs, having written down the address, wanted to get him off the line, but Mr Simmonds kept talking.

'Naylor was a lonely boy,' he said. 'I thought about him. Your visit set my mind to remembering him. He was what you people call a loner. It's odd that he should have affection for the old school, but I suppose it represents, at least in his mind, a time when he belonged. But of course he didn't.'

It was gone seven o'clock when Hobbs put the phone down and drove to the village where Naylor lived. It came as a surprise to find he lived there. It was only three miles from Salthaven but it was a peaceful rural village. Hobbs had the usual prejudices of the police. Although he would never use the expression, he believed in the 'criminal classes'. He saw crime starting with poverty and under-privilege. But then, rape did not spring from poverty. It came from something else altogether.

The village had a Norman church, a post office which was also the local shop, and an old manor house, now divided into flats. In Salthaven they sold postcards of the place to tourists looking for sites of local interest.

He found the house he wanted, one of a row of tiny terraced cottages facing the church.

Mrs Smith answered the door and said her son hadn't been home all day. She looked like one of those respectable women who are haughty to policemen, but Hobbs could see she was frightened having him at the door.

'What's Terry done now?' she asked.

She looked on the verge of tears. Hobbs said he hadn't done anything as far as he knew. But she didn't believe it.

'I never know what's he's going to do next. He had a girl in his room — he's very good-looking, such a handsome boy — and he just went out and left her here. It was very embarrassing for me. She was a nice enough girl, I suppose, but not his sort at all, only a waitress in a café near the docks.'

'Bert's Café?'

'That's right. I thought how common it sounded when she told me. Her name's Mary.' The thought of a new horror struck her. She said, 'Nothing's happened to her, has it?'

Hobbs tried to reassure her.

'No, no. It's nothing,' he said.

Her manner then changed. 'If it's nothing, Officer, why have you come here so late? He was innocent, you know. He was found not guilty. It did terrible things to him, being an innocent young man in prison on remand for three months. You're a young man yourself. You should know how some of these girls are, what they'll say to get themselves noticed if a good-looking boy doesn't want to have anything to do with them. And now you're hounding him.'

Finally he escaped.

It was getting dusk by the time he got to Bert's Café.

Mary was clearing tables.

'Do you know Terry Naylor?' Hobbs asked.

'Has there been an accident?' She looked worried.

He asked why she thought there might

have been an accident.

'He was upset about something. I shouted after him but he didn't come back. He didn't even turn round to look at me.'

'Was he going in the direction of the marina?'

'What? Yes. He goes there a lot. He loves the sea. He's got a friend with a big boat there.'

Hobbs drove to the marina. The wind was getting up. There was a crowd of reporters at the marina gates, pressing against the link chain fence. Hobbs saw the journalist who had taken the picture of Fiona Farr and Bruce Wheeler. He knew Pearson. They had been to school together.

Pearson came up smiling and said, 'Hello, Billy. Looks like Salthaven has missed out on the great rape.'

'How'd you know Bruce Wheeler was on that boat?'

'I didn't. I thought it was the Venerable Tom.'

'So who told you?'

'Professional secret.'

'Who told you?'

'You know I can't reveal my sources.'

'Your sources won't help you when you're arrested.'

'Arrested for what?'

'There's plenty I could fit you up for.'

'You're not that kind of cop.'

'Maybe I've suddenly become that kind of cop.'

'It's no skin off my nose, Billy,' Pearson said. 'His name's Terry Naylor. That's all I know.'

Hobbs knew now where Naylor was. He was certain that Naylor was stalking the women. He went towards the locked gates and rattled them until the nightwatchman came grumbling out of his hut.

'Are you Press?'

'No,' Hobbs said, 'police.'

Old Ted unlocked the gate. Hobbs showed him the photo of Naylor.

'What's he done?' Ted asked.

'Never mind what he's done. Have you seen him?'

'He was here but he's gone. He was going to look after things for me but he buggered off.'

'Which is Fiona Farr's berth?'

'Thirty-six,' Ted said. 'Down there.'

Hobbs ran along the pontoon to the berth. But the *Eumenides* was gone.

27

The headland off the starboard bow seemed to be on fire. A narrow streak of orange sky above the outline of the land looked like a band of flame, with great dark banks of cloud like smoke billowing across the blackening sky. The wind, which had been blowing a stiff breeze as they came out of the marina, was getting stronger. Fiona and Clem had to shout to each other to be heard above the clap of canvas and the sound of water breaking over the bow.

Fiona was at the tiller. Last time I did this, she thought, Bruce Wheeler was with me. I could have become his mistress. She considered the old-fashioned word. It meant a man kept a girl in a flat in London and put money in her bank account. That wouldn't be enough for me, she said to herself. Then she could feel herself going hot with embarrassment thinking about the mess she had created. Thank God he hit me and left me a bruise when he thought I'd set him up, she thought. I've got to protect myself. And he did rape me. He did. It's rape when you say stop and they don't. It doesn't matter what you've said or done before. He should have stopped. And then she thought, that wasn't rape, it was enthusiastic consensual lust, but I'm the only one in the world who knows it. Except for him. Or does he think that what he did was rape? His father believed he was a rapist. He must, or he wouldn't resign; he'd fight. With all his money, he'd be bound to win in the end. Another rotten father, Fiona told herself, he just wants to keep out of it. But, she thought, it's time I stopped living dangerously. That little gamble nearly cost me my career.

She turned to Clem. Clem was sitting in the front corner of the cockpit, her long legs braced across the top of the companionway. She had the hood of her oilskin pulled up over her short hair. Her face shone in the light from the navigation desk below. But the boat tugged like a big dog on a lead. Fiona had to screw up her eyes to see what was happening as the spray stung her sore face. She didn't have time for conversation with Clem, and it looked as though it might get even more lively once they were out of the bay beyond Studholme Island. Fiona loved this kind of sailing, with the boat skimming through the water and the sails tight to the wind, and herself with the power of the sea and the wind in her hand.

The boat sped through the dark water, foam creamed along the side-deck as she heeled; a sail, the big jib, blotted out the flame-topped headland as Fiona headed off the wind. They'd got too much sail up; they'd have to take the big number one jib down, it was too much.

Clem leaned out of the cockpit to peer ahead under the sail. She tried to say something, but the wind whipped the words out of her mouth; for a moment she could not breathe. She looked up at Fiona. Fiona was wearing a woollen hat pulled down over her long dark hair. In the growing dark her bruised face was pale against the glittering golden lights of Salthaven far behind. Clem thought there was something supernatural about Fiona's face, the colour of gleaming bone, with the dark eye sockets empty in the gloomy light. Out here at sea, amid the crashing waves and the keening wind, ordinary life seemed to have been suspended. The boat began to buck and pitch as she met the open sea outside the headland. She could see Fiona putting all her weight against the tiller to hold their course. The wind was still increasing and becoming blustery.

'We'd better change down,' Fiona shouted.

Clem stood up, holding on to the edge of the hatch. 'Number two jib?' she asked.

Fiona said, 'Can you bring up the safety lines while you're at it? They're all in the sail locker.'

Clem disappeared down the companionway. Fiona reached forward and eased the jib sheet a little. The effect was to cut the boat's speed and increase the noise. The sail cracked like a series of explosions. Fiona wished Marjorie was with them. Sail changes were easier with three, and they were going to have to put at least one reef in the mainsail.

The wind took on a new, hysterical note. They were going to have real trouble if they didn't get that sail changed.

'Clem,' Fiona shouted, 'what the hell are you doing down there?'

There was no answer. Fiona leaned forward and peered down the companionway. She dared not move too far in case the tiller leaped out of her grip. 'Clem,' she shouted again, 'get a move on.'

The light on the navigation desk disappeared. That meant Clem must be blocking it as she made her way back to the cockpit. About time too, Fiona thought.

Fiona was too busy to look as Clem came up the ladder. She was concentrating on searching the horizon off the port bow for the flashing light of the next buoy.

'What took so damned long?' she said.

'We're going to have to hurry.'

There was no answer. Clem seemed to be standing there doing nothing.

'Get on with it,' Fiona said. 'Secure the safety line before you go forward and yell when you're ready to drop the number one.'

Naylor said, 'Do it yourself. I'm not the hired hand.'

Fiona was too shocked at first to be frightened. The boat veered off the wind with an explosion of canvas. She didn't recognize the man standing there.

Naylor stood framed in the cabin hatch as she pulled the boat back on course. She did not know who he was but he reminded her of someone. He was not dressed for sailing in this weather. His old sweater was already drenched. His lank hair was plastered to his head. He had a gold ring in one ear. She thought he might be a reporter who had stowed away.

'It's pretty rough, isn't it?' she said. 'You must be sorry you came. I'm Fiona. Who are you?'

He stepped over the cabin lintel and into the cockpit. She could see the open pores on the skin of his forehead.

'You know who I am,' he said. 'You know I've been here before. On this boat with you and your friends.'

He thrust his face into hers and she did remember. She felt weak in the wrists and her legs went limp. The tiller was trying to leap out of her hands and she felt too weak to stop it. She saw the axe tucked through his belt loop.

'Where's Clem?' she asked.

'I've dealt with her.'

He grabbed the collar of her oilskin and tore it open. Buttons from her blouse fell on the deck.

'You remember now?' he asked.

She nodded. She could feel his breath on her face. She could see no way out. He had come to kill her. He had probably killed Clem already.

She was not thinking about what she was doing. It was almost as though the yacht took a hand and turned suddenly so that the wind went out of the mainsail, and the long metal boom swung like a scythe across the cockpit before the sail filled again. The larger jib, held to the starboard side by the tightly winched sheet, tried to turn inside out, but came up against the wire stays holding the mast upright. The canvas raged like something in a trap. The boom narrowly missed Naylor's head. It glanced his shoulder and threw him sideways. Fiona hauled the tiller across to bring the boat round on their original course so that the boom swung back again and the jib filled.

'We've got to lighten sail,' Fiona screamed at Naylor. 'We've had it if we don't. Can you do it?'

Naylor, looking greenish, picked himself up from the well of the cockpit and crouched in the shelter of the cabin bulkhead. 'Go up there?' he yelled back. 'In this weather, with you at the helm ready to swing her round again and let the sail knock me into the sea? I'm not daft.'

'OK, OK, just go up there and undo the clip to bring the sail down, and I'll go below and pull the big jib in through the forward hatch. We won't put the number two up.'

'No,' he said, 'I don't want you to go down there.' He looked around. A gust made the boat suddenly heel. Sea water surged over the cabin roof and swamped the cockpit. She could see he was frightened now. He knew they had to do something.

'I'll go below,' he said. 'You go and undo the sail. And no funny stuff. I've got this axe.' He put his hand to the axe.

'What have you done to her?' Fiona imagined the cabin spattered with Clem's blood. But he turned away and went below. She saw the flap of the forehatch open. He was in the sail locker ready to drag the wet sail through from the deck as it came down. At that moment the boat dipped into a wall of water which broke over the foredeck and gushed through the open hatch. At least he got another drenching, she thought.

I'll kill him if I get the chance, she thought, but I'll have to take the body right out to sea and weight it down where no one will find it before the fish have eaten away those whiplash marks on his back.

She brought the boat round into the wind. Then she pulled the cords attached to the deckrails and looped them round the tiller to keep the boat steady. Moving as carefully as she could on the streaming, bucking deck, she went forward to release the jib halyard.

The sail fought all the way. She knelt on the heaving deck trying to control the wet canvas. The tips of her fingers burned as she tried to get a grip on it. Naylor was hauling at the slack from below, dragging it through the hatch into the sail locker.

She fed the last of the canvas down to him and dropped the hatch. Making her way back to the cockpit she had to cling to the handrail on the cabin roof. She paused, leaning against the bulwark. Then she took a deep breath and made her way back to the tiller, expecting she didn't know what.

Naylor came staggering up the companion

ladder. She could not take her eyes off the axe in his belt. In the cockpit he slumped in the corner. He was pale, and sweating. He was breathless. He was seasick. If I'd got something to hit him with, I could kill him now, she thought.

'I've got to put a reef in the mainsail,' she shouted at him. 'We've still got too much canvas.' It was extraordinary, she thought, listening to herself giving a running commentary like this to the man. He nodded his head.

Even with the boat headed into the wind, Fiona had to struggle to ease the mainsail down enough to fold the streaming canvas for the reef. At last she made the row of short wet cords on the sail fast round the boom. She clambered back into the cockpit and rested her head on her arms against the tiller, breathing hard.

'You're playing for time,' he said.

'Don't be stupid,' she said. 'Look at me, you bastard. Can't you see what I've done single-handed to keep us from going under and letting a bastard like you drown? Anyway, where the fuck are you in such a hurry to go?'

'Out to sea,' he said. He had the axe in his hand but then he pushed the handle back through the belt loop.

'Out to sea? Isn't this enough fucking sea for you?'

'Make for France,' he said. 'I fancy a new life in France.'

'Where's Clem? What have you done to Clem? You don't recognize her, do you?'

'I know what she did, her and your old fat friend.'

He didn't recognize Clem as his victim, the one who'd fought back. It threw Fiona off-guard. She asked quickly, 'What are you going to do with me?'

As soon as she'd asked, she wished she hadn't.

'You don't know what I'm going to do with you,' he said. 'Maybe I'll dump you and the other one overboard.'

'You can't sail the boat by yourself. You'd never get into a French harbour on your own.'

'Oh,' he said, 'that won't be a problem. I'll make for the shore and then put the outboard in the dinghy and abandon ship. I'll get ashore in the dinghy.'

'The dinghy's not on board.'

'I don't believe you,' he said.

She could see he was supremely confident, as though nothing he did could go wrong; except he started getting green again. The boat was pitching badly. He looked less threatening. 'It wasn't fair,' he said, 'what you did to me.'

'It wasn't fair what you did,' Fiona said.

'What you did to me was worse than that. Don't try telling me you and me aren't the same, taking what we want when we get the chance. That's the difference between us and losers.' Then he added, 'Except it's a question of the survival of the fittest now, and this time it's my turn. You're the loser now.'

Fiona released the tiller and turned the boat until the truncated mainsail filled. They began to move again. The yacht was much easier to handle. They no longer galloped through the water like a bolting horse. Fiona looked at Naylor. He still looked sick. He tried to pull the sleeves of the ragged old sweater down over his damp red hands.

Very slowly, almost imperceptibly, she brought the boat round so that they were heading along the coast, no longer out to sea.

'Are you afraid?' Naylor suddenly asked.

'Afraid of you? You're kidding. I despise you. It's such a bloody waste to be killed by a piece of shit like you. I'm ambitious. I'd hoped for something better than being finished off by a fucking low-life.'

'You,' he said, 'you're not normal, going round flogging men, throwing a man in the sea to drown. You're the one who's crazy. I got all the evidence I need on my back. I could have you put away. I don't have to kill you.' He leaned towards her. 'Why don't you ask me nicely?'

'Beg, you mean? Like you did?'

'You'll beg. I'll make you beg.'

She ignored him. She was too confident, he didn't like that. It was as though she actually believed that in spite of everything she was in charge. But she thought he had killed her friend. That was good, he'd let her go on thinking that. All he'd done was truss her up good. He'd taken her by surprise. He hadn't had to hit her hard. He didn't want to kill her. Not yet. Or this one. This little power cunt wasn't going to escape that easy. It was her fault. She would fight, though, when it came to it, that would be good. He was looking forward to this one. He could tell he disgusted her. She'd be a lot more disgusted when she realized there was nothing she could do about it, that she was in his power.

'I saw the pictures,' he said, 'you've got nice tits.'

'You're sick,' Fiona said. 'You should be locked up.'

'Me sick?' he said. 'You're the one that's sick.'

'A woman has the right to fight back. We had a right to make you pay.'

She stood there casually talking as if he were someone annoying her in a pub. Naylor leaned forward and suddenly grabbed her ankles, jerking her off the cockpit bench.

'You owe me,' he said. 'I've suffered. I've got the right to compensation.'

She tried to kick but her feet slipped against the wet floor. She landed on her knees in the well.

He stepped round her and took the tiller. She was facing him, still not saying a word or making a sound, looking superior as though she was thinking he was scum.

'What you did to me,' he said, 'I couldn't sleep for months after what you did to me.' But she only stared at him with her white face with no interest as if he did not exist. 'Come here,' he said, 'let's see those tits that were on TV.'

But she did not react properly. She undid her shirt. She was showing them to him, kneeling with her shirt pulled open and her tits sticking out. She didn't even have a contemptuous look on her face, there was no expression there at all. When he reached out and felt them she didn't back away or flinch. She remained on her knees staring at him with that blank swollen face.

'How about this?' he said.

With his free hand he grabbed her woolly hat and pulled it off. He took a fistful of her thick black hair and wrenched her head forward. When she tried to turn her head away he smiled, she was disgusted now, he was getting a response. He released the tiller to open his trousers. He could hear her trying to breathe. Then she bit him hard. He doubled up and went to smack her across the head to make her stop but when he did he let go of her hair and she scrambled through the hatch into the cabin, slamming the door at the top of the companionway shut behind her.

He heard the bolt slide across. He tried to go after her, but the pain was too much. He sprawled across the cockpit. He could feel the blood gushing.

Fiona stumbled down the companionway. She grabbed the edge of the berth to break her fall and touched warm skin.

Clem was lying on the berth. Her hands were tied with the safety lines and she had been gagged with a tea towel. Fiona pulled the gag from Clem's mouth.

'Are you all right?' she asked. Her own head was ringing from when Naylor had hit her and there was blood in her mouth, but it wasn't her blood. She spat and started to untie Clem's bonds. She could hear Naylor raging with pain in the cockpit.

'What's happening?' Clem said. She looked terrified.

Fiona was too busy to answer. She found a sharp kitchen knife in the galley and sawed at the cords round Clem's wrists. Naylor had tied them so tight they were cutting into the flesh.

They could hear Naylor howling above the sound of the wind. The boat was out of control, wallowing in the heavy swell, then pitching at a steep angle back and forth. Fiona had to be careful with the knife as Clem was tipped this way and that as the yacht reared and dived.

'There,' Fiona said as Clem's wrists were free. 'Do your own ankles. I've got to get on the radio.'

There was a crash above their heads.

'He's breaking through the hatch,' Clem said, looking up from where she sat sawing at the cords round her ankles. 'I think he's got an axe.'

Fiona was crouched over the navigation table, working the knobs on the boat's radio. Splinters of wood fell round her on to the charts as she shouted 'Mayday, Mayday' into the radio. Behind her in the cabin Clem was on her feet, stamping to bring the circulation back. Then the head of Naylor's axe broke through the panel above her head. The next blow would smash the lock. The radio crackled and hissed. Fiona shouted again,

'Mayday, Mayday.'

Then the hatch was slammed back. She looked up and saw Naylor's face only inches away leaning down over her. He raised the axe to strike at her. As he did the boat heeled and the weakened wood gave way under his weight. Fiona leaped back as he crashed down the companionway.

She felt Clem grab her from behind and pull her back. 'Quick,' Clem said, 'into the sail locker.'

Naylor grasped the edge of the navigation table to pull himself to his feet, but he had to struggle with the movement of the boat. He lunged forward. Clem fell backwards through the slatted door of the sail locker, pulling Fiona down with her on to the wet canvas of the big jib piled there. Fiona kicked the door shut behind her and bolted it. They lay in a heap on the wet sail to get their breath back. They could hear Naylor groan and curse outside the door.

'We haven't got long,' Fiona said. 'He'll be through that door in no time. We've got to get on deck through the forehatch. Then he'll have to catch us.'

Naylor stopped groaning. They waited, trying to listen. There was no sound.

'What's he doing?' Clem asked. She was whispering in Fiona's ear as if she was afraid

Naylor might hear.

Fiona tried to see into the cabin through the slats in the door. 'I can't see anything,' she said. As she turned her head back to Clem, the blade of Naylor's axe crashed through the wood where her eye had been.

'No time,' Clem cried, and she threw back the forehatch and pulled herself through on to the deck. She leaned back in and reached down for Fiona's hand to help her climb through.

'I'll kill him if he climbs through after us,' Fiona said. She had the kitchen knife. She held it up. The blade looked ridiculously short against a man with an axe. 'There's the flare gun in the locker,' she said. 'I'll get that too.' She turned to climb back down into the sail locker.

'Don't,' Clem said. 'He's coming through.' They could hear Naylor smashing the axe against the inside door.

'We've got to do something,' Fiona said. She lowered herself back through the forehatch. Naylor hit the inside door again. The head of the axe appeared through the wood. The door was giving way. Fiona could see Naylor's face through the smashed wood. She grabbed the flare gun from its shelf and Clem helped as she pulled herself back through the hatch on to the deck. Clem slammed the hatch cover down behind her.

'Thank God, it's loaded,' Fiona said, checking the gun. 'But there's only one shot. The spares are in the cockpit.' She sat down panting for breath, and only then looked down and saw her shirt was unbuttoned and her breasts hanging out.

'We should fire the flare for help,' Clem said.

'Who'll see? Who'll get here in time?'

The noise of Naylor battering at the door stopped. Maybe he's passed out, or bled to death, Fiona thought. She started to button her shirt but the boat rocked crazily. They had to cling to the mast stepping to stop themselves sliding across the deck.

Fiona saw the distant lights of Salthaven somersault as the boat plunged into another black wall of water. The wave broke over the bow and swamped her. She managed to grab a stay as she was whirled along the deck. Clem was wedged between the deckrail and the cabin bulkhead.

'Could you really use it?' Clem shouted, pointing at the flare gun in Fiona's hands. 'Could you shoot him with it?'

'You bet I'll use it. I bit his cock off, didn't I?'

'Jesus,' Clem said, 'you did what?'

'I bit his cock. I bit right through it. I hope

he's bleeding to death. It gives us a chance.'

Then the sea eased for a moment after its show of strength. The boat steadied. The full moon came out from behind a cloud, turning a ghostly spotlight on the yacht. They listened but they could hear no sound from Naylor.

'Where do you think he is?' Clem asked. 'What's he doing?'

'Perhaps he's passed out from loss of blood. I hope he's lying there dying.'

They kept their eyes on the forehatch waiting for the man to appear. Then they heard him roar. He was behind them in the cockpit, brandishing the axe. He wavered for a moment. Then he began to move slowly towards them along the side deck.

'Holy shit,' Fiona said, 'this is it.'

She raised the flare gun in both hands.

'Oh, my God,' Clem said. She closed her eyes; she couldn't look.

There was a flash. The flare missed Naylor. It hit the metal mast and ricocheted. Fiona saw it falling in a shower of sparks. She saw Naylor crouched in the cockpit.

'Shit,' Fiona said. Then she heard the screams of pain. He was on fire. The flare had landed on him. His sweater burned as though it had been soaked in petrol.

'Oh, God,' Clem said.

They watched as he staggered, bent double

with the flames engulfing his back. Fiona moved forward to see. Naylor was down, rolling desperately on the cockpit floor trying to put out the flames, screaming all the time for them to help him. The cockpit was awash with the water they had shipped. The flames hissed and went out. They could hear Naylor whimpering in the dark.

Fiona raised the empty flare gun. 'I've got to get past him to the spares,' she said.

'You can't,' Clem said.

'I won't miss next time,' Fiona said. 'Then we'll have to take him out and dump him.'

'What?' Clem couldn't believe her ears.

But then the boat was bathed in a harsh light. There was the sound of a powerful engine. They saw the outline of the big coastguard boat, black behind the glare of the spotlight. A man shouted through a megaphone.

Fiona said, 'Now we're for it.'

Clem did not understand. 'Why?' she asked. 'He stowed away and tried to kill us.'

'He'll talk,' Fiona said. 'He said he'd talk.'

The coastguard boat came alongside. Two men climbed on board the yacht.

'My God,' one of them said, 'what happened here?'

28

The weather had returned to something more like summer when Hobbs went to the hospital to see Fiona Farr and Clementine Illingworth. Naylor was going to live, but his burns were horrific. He had been rushed back to Salthaven in the coastguard cutter, leaving one of the crew on board the *Eumenides* to help the two women bring her back to harbour.

What Fiona Farr did to Naylor had caused a few laughs in the station but it wasn't really much to laugh at. And given the burns the man had suffered, he would be scarred for life. It was another thing for Fiona Farr to live down. She'd already got quite a name for herself in the scandal about Bruce Wheeler and now this had happened. She was a celebrity, but, Hobbs supposed, not the sort of celebrity she'd want to be. When he came into her room in the hospital she didn't look much of a star. She had a swollen eye as well as the previous bruising, and Naylor seemed to have pulled out clumps of her hair. A police photographer had already taken pictures of

249

the damage to be used as evidence.

Mrs Warren was in the room with Fiona Farr and Clementine. They were sitting close together talking in low, urgent voices. They stopped when he came in. Mrs Warren rose and stood as if she were protecting the two younger women against further attack. There was something gallant about them, he thought, especially with the two young women showing the marks of having been through the wars. Mrs Warren, the way she stood alongside them, made it look as if it was a photograph of two generations of triumphant womanhood. Yesterday Mrs Warren had been nervous. She wasn't nervous now. She was holding her head up looking at him across the room. Her chin was raised so that she looked like the picture he had seen of her before her daughter disappeared.

'What do you want, Constable?' she asked.

Hobbs was surprised that she was the one who spoke up like that, as though she spoke for them all. Mrs Warren had been the one he expected would crack. He hadn't been able to see her getting carried away by such a great sense of injustice that she would take the law into her own hands, not a respectable middle-aged lady like that; but now he saw that he had been wrong. Maybe her daughter's disappearance had changed her.

Her world had been thrown off its axis, and she was off kilter too. It was as though a lifetime's process of emotional evolution had been compressed into no time at all. It was something new, Hobbs thought. Women like Mrs Warren were not the criminal classes; they had crimes committed against them, they were mugged, they had their houses broken into, they even had their daughters raped and murdered, but they didn't commit crimes, not until now. Hobbs asked himself what had happened to make the difference. Once women like that just talked about bringing back hanging and flogging, they approved of vengeful justice, even castration. It was a worrying thought for the police if women like Marjorie Warren had finally decided they could look after themselves better than the institutions they had always trusted to do it for them.

'I've come to tell Miss Farr and Miss Illingworth that we've finished here. As far as we're concerned they're free to leave,' he said to Mrs Warren, as if Fiona Farr and Clem weren't there.

'I've come to take Clem home,' Mrs Warren said. 'The doctor wants Fiona to stay in overnight.'

'Do you feel up to it?' Hobbs asked Clem. 'Yes,' she said. 'Thank you.'

Hobbs left them. He went to see Naylor. A uniformed man was on duty outside the door of his room.

'What's going on?' Hobbs asked.

'The inspector talked to him earlier,' the uniformed man said. 'He didn't get much out of him though. He said Naylor was raving. He kept saying he'd been whipped and had the scars to prove it. He's going to have scars all right. He's got bad burns all over his back, poor sod. And that other thing, well, that's something else. I'd sooner be dead myself. Did they find it?'

'What?' Hobbs asked, but he knew what the uniformed man was talking about.

'They could sew it back on,' the uniformed man said, 'bit late, though, even if they found it.'

'It didn't get bitten right off,' Hobbs said.

'It didn't?' The uniformed man sounded as if he thought Hobbs was spoiling a good story. 'Well, he's all right then. I won't waste my sympathy.'

'Anyone in there with him now?' Hobbs asked.

'He's supposed to be left alone.'

'I only want five minutes,' Hobbs said.

'I need a slash,' the uniformed man said. 'You can sneak in, but make it quick.'

Naylor was lying on his stomach on a kind

of inflated plastic bag. He was conscious. Hobbs squatted by the bed so that his face was close to Naylor's. Naylor couldn't raise his head but the eye nearest Hobbs turned to look at him.

'Why did you do it? What have you got against those women?' Hobbs asked.

He had to lean close to hear Naylor's answer.

'They whipped the shit out of me,' Naylor said. 'Like that other one, the body on the beach. Look at my back if you don't believe me. I've got the whip marks, same as the man on the beach. They drowned him. They're killers.'

Hobbs stood up and looked. There was no sign of whip lashes on Naylor's back. There was no skin at all, only ugly raw flesh. Hobbs thought he was going to be sick. It's a wonder he's going to live, Hobbs thought.

'They'll go to prison,' Naylor said. 'Taking the law into their own hands, they deserve to.' His voice seemed to be coming from a long way off. 'At least I've put them in prison.'

The poor bastard, Hobbs thought, he wasn't going to put anyone anywhere. The evidence was all burned up. Hobbs squatted down by the side of the bed, but this time Naylor didn't look at him.

'I got them, right?'

Hobbs thought it was probably his moral duty to make the poor bastard feel better. 'That's right,' he said. Then he got up and left.

The uniformed man had returned to his post outside the door.

'OK?' he asked when Hobbs came out.

'He's fine,' Hobbs said, 'but he's delirious.'

'At least he got it back,' the uniformed man said. 'I was standing there taking a slash and I kept thinking the poor bastard, at least he's got it back.'

Hobbs walked slowly down the corridor towards Fiona Farr's room. When he knocked at the door Mrs Warren's voice told him to come in.

Fiona Farr was out of bed, wearing a sweater and jeans. Mrs Warren was collecting her things and putting them into a suitcase. Clementine Illingworth sat stiffly in the chair provided for visitors.

'I thought they were keeping you in?' Hobbs said to Fiona Farr.

'I'm going home,' she said. 'I've checked myself out.'

Hobbs said, 'I've just been talking to Naylor.'

There was a short silence. Then Mrs Warren said, 'Well? What did he have to say for himself?'

Hobbs spoke as though only to Fiona. He said, 'Naylor says you flogged him.'

They looked at each other, then back at him. Fiona Farr smiled. 'Did he?' she said. 'And why should he say that?'

'He said he got on to you because you did the same thing to Martin Bakewell.'

No one spoke. Marjorie Warren snapped the suitcase shut. If Hobbs was hoping they would break down and confess he was mistaken.

'Let's get you home, young lady,' Mrs Warren said to Fiona. 'Clem, you take this.' She handed Clem the suitcase. Then she looked Hobbs straight in the eye. 'I suppose we can go?' she said. 'You're not arresting us, are you?'

Hobbs shook his head. 'I'm making an investigation,' he said. 'I know where to find you.' He turned and left the room.

At the station Sergeant Howard came up to him and asked, 'How's it going? Naylor charged yet?'

Hobbs nodded. 'It'll be some time before he's fit to appear in court. We've got him on assault and actual bodily harm so far. But those girls weren't really hurt. He's the one who got hurt.'

'Serves him right,' Sergeant Howard said. 'We got him for kidnapping and attempted murder.'

'He says the women were vigilantes who flogged him. He says he's got scars on his back to prove it.'

'And has he got scars on his back to prove it?'

'We'll never know,' Hobbs said. 'All the skin on his back was burned away.'

'Case dismissed,' Sergeant Howard said.

Hobbs thought of the kid at the marina whose mother had complained to Greene about Naylor. Greene hadn't looked at Naylor's back. He didn't even make a report at the time, he'd been too busy getting ready to go to Canada to become a central-heating engineer.

'Naylor mentioned the Bakewell case,' Hobbs said.

'Does he think a story like that's going to get him off in court?'

'But suppose he's telling the truth?'

Sergeant Howard was impatient. 'Did Naylor attack those two women?'

'Yes.'

'Can you prove it beyond reasonable doubt?'

'Yes.'

'Will you get a conviction?'

'Yes.'

'Right. Good. Now, are those three respectable women a vigilante group? Can you prove they are?'

Hobbs hesitated. He was about to say 'I think they are' but he found he could not say the words. He said, 'Terry Naylor says so.'

'Is *Mister* Naylor a reliable witness?'

'No.'

'Does *Mister* Naylor have any evidence to prove his accusations?'

'No.'

'Can you prove those women attacked and flogged Naylor and the body you found in the estuary?'

'No.'

'Are they going to confess?'

Hobbs thought of the way the three women had looked at him when he told them Naylor had accused them. Hobbs knew he wasn't going to break those women down. And I'm not sure I want to, he thought. He said to Sergeant Howard, 'Not at the moment.'

'Not ever,' Sergeant Howard said. 'Do you think you're ever going to convince a jury that those women banded together to form some sort of sex terrorist group? There's enough crime without creating it where it doesn't exist.'

He's right, Hobbs thought, it's time I moved on from this.

Sergeant Howard gave Hobbs a friendly clout on the shoulder. 'Don't take it all so hard, son,' he said. 'You've done your job. Terry Naylor'll be banged up for a good long time. That's all you're paid for, to take villains off the street. Protect the victims. If you want the other thing, be a social worker. No, better than that, be a priest, a Catholic priest. Then they actually come and confess their crimes to you, but you can't arrest them. You can't do anything but forgive them. Maybe you'd like that. Maybe that'd be right up your street.'

29

Marjorie could hear the postman grumbling outside the front door.

'Just listen to him complaining,' Marjorie said. 'As if we don't have a right to complain. After all, we're the ones who have to read that stuff.'

'If we *did* read it,' Clem said. Some time ago they'd stopped reading the letters that came through the post from strangers.

Marjorie watched as further envelopes fell on to the heap on the mat.

Six months ago Terry Naylor had been well enough to stand up in the witness box. He'd accused the three of them, Fiona, Clem and Marjorie, of being vigilantes who avenged women by flogging men. It had been sensational.

Terry Naylor's own lawyer had tried to stop him. The judge had been very stern and told the jury to ignore what Naylor had just said. But Naylor took no notice. He began shouting. He tore the shirt off his back and showed his terrible scars. He was hysterical. Marjorie had cringed seeing the state of him. Everyone in the courtroom cringed. He pointed at Fiona and said she had flayed the skin off his back. It was all nonsense, of course. The court had heard about his horrible burns.

But the newspapers got excited. Some took the trouble to check with the police afterwards and they found there were no inquiries being made into female vigilantes, that there was no evidence, and that there would be no charges. But it was such a good story that some newspapers couldn't resist, and under the guise of showing how mad Terry Naylor was, one of the broadsheets called the three women 'The Furies', after the avengers of mythology. The reporter was a graduate trainee and he wanted to show off that he knew that in Greek mythology the Furies were called the Eumenides. 'That was the name of their boat,' he told the sub-editor, who grumbled, but he thought it was a nice coincidence and he let it stand. Then the tabloids dragged up what had been written about Clem as Miss X when she was raped; they dug up everything that had happened to Tessa Warren and speculated about how this would affect a mother's state of mind. And Fiona, of course, had only recently been involved in the scandal of the resignation of the former political adviser to the Prime Minister. She had accused his son of rape. The reporters projected Fiona as the beautiful siren who lured men to their punishment. Fiona didn't seem to mind that at all. Marjorie could see her acting up to the image being created for her by the gutter Press. Marjorie stopped speaking to Fiona. Or she would have done if she'd come face to face with her.

The trouble was there was no let up when the court case finished and Naylor was sent to prison. Here it was, six months later and the post was still piled high against Marjorie's front door. There were also still many annoying telephone calls. Marjorie had an answering machine installed and kept it switched on even when she was in the house.

Naturally, at first, she and Clem *had* opened the letters.

'What do these women want us to do?' Clem said.

'Kill men for them,' Marjorie said.

When it went on and on they put all the letters unopened into black plastic sacks and shoved them in a cupboard. Marjorie said she would look at them some time. And she intended to do so. She didn't like to pass the cupboard where the plastic bags were.

They had not been able to silence the telephone so easily. They played back messages requesting speeches, comments, interviews, personal appearances, and also offers of support and the names of many men who needed a good flogging. Those were the nice calls. There were others that were full of abuse. Not all from men, there were abusive calls from women too. Some women hated them.

During all this, they never saw Fiona. She didn't come to the Fitness Centre. They no longer went sailing with her.

One morning Clem said, 'Fiona's left her job.'

'I don't wonder they wanted to get rid of her,' Marjorie said.

'I don't think they sacked her. Why wait this long if they wanted to fire her?'

'So it wouldn't get them a bad name.'

'No,' Clem said, 'I know she quit. One of the men she used to work with has started coming to the gym. Did she ever mention anyone called Tim Yates? He said they were going to get married but apparently it all went wrong.

'In his dreams,' Marjorie said. It was what Fiona would have said. Clem laughed.

'No, I didn't believe it either,' she said. 'I think he's had some sort of breakdown. A lot of people who come to the gym really just want someone to talk to.'

Yes, Marjorie thought, I know they do.

That's how all this started.

Clem went on, 'This Tim Yates said she'd quit. She's gone to London. She's got herself a new job. She's on television. She's presenting an afternoon show.'

'I've never seen her.'

'Well, we never watch. Do you know who else is on the show?'

'How would I know, dear?' Marjorie was patient.

'Bruce Wheeler,' Clem said.

'I don't believe it.' Marjorie was shocked. But then she laughed. 'She's incredible, isn't she?' she said.

'Apparently Bruce Wheeler suggested it,' Clem said. 'He feels guilty she got involved when he was set up. He's decided she didn't know what was going on. He's put it all down to a tabloid plot to discredit his father.'

'But she accused him of rape,' Marjorie said.

Clem shrugged.

'Is she any good on television?' Silly question, Marjorie thought, of course Fiona would be good on television.

'Search me,' Clem said. 'Tim Yates isn't exactly a dispassionate critic. He says he can't bear to watch her.' She paused, and then said in a tentative way as though she wasn't sure how Marjorie would react, 'Fiona's pregnant.

She's going to have a baby.'

'I know what pregnant means,' Marjorie said. 'Who's the father?'

'Tim doesn't know that. I think he wishes it was his.'

Marjorie wasn't sure how she felt about this. She didn't expect ever to meet Fiona again. But there was also an odd compulsion to see her, to see how she looked, how she was with Bruce Wheeler, how he was with her.

Marjorie had altogether different feelings about Clem. After Naylor's trial she realized that she no longer looked forward to the day when Clem would find herself somewhere of her own to live. She no longer found her sulky. She was even prepared to put up with visits from Detective Constable Hobbs, who was constantly driving by, he said, and thought he'd call in to see how they were doing.

Marjorie went into the kitchen to make a pot of camomile tea. While she waited for the kettle to boil she called to Clem in the other room, 'We must watch that show of Fiona's.'

There was no answer and when Clem came into the kitchen a few minutes later Marjorie noticed that she looked flushed. She kept her eyes fixed on the floor. She had that old sullen look she'd had when she first moved in.

'I've just made a phone call,' she said.

'You don't have to ask permission,' Marjorie said. 'Make all the calls you want.' But she knew this was not really what Clem meant.

'No,' Clem said, 'I called home.'

'Home?'

'My Mum.'

Marjorie didn't know what to say. She knew how important this was for Clem, but her throat ached. She knew now that Clem was going to leave her. Marjorie could see herself alone again, sinking into that old gloom she had been sunk in for so long, and had only just started to climb out of. But she must not let Clem see any of this, she must be brave and caring.

When she recovered her breath she asked, 'How do you feel?'

Clem kept her head down. She didn't answer the question directly. 'Mum sounded just the same,' she said, 'as though nothing had happened, except she couldn't stop crying. But Dad's ill. I said I'd go and see him. But maybe I should stay and take care of him. Mum's not strong.'

Marjorie wanted to cry out, 'I love you,' but she couldn't speak. 'Here,' she said, 'drink the tea. It's getting cold.'

The next day she drove Clem to the train.

It had been snowing and it was very cold. On the platform, Clem hugged her. 'Was it wrong, what we did?' she asked.

Marjorie shrugged. 'I don't know. Lots of things are wrong and right at he same time. Women shouldn't have to be afraid.'

After the train left Marjorie thought she should have said they meant well. That was an excuse.

The house was very quiet when she got home. She opened the door of Clem's room. The bed was made, not stripped. Nothing much was packed. Marjorie smiled. She was touched. Clem had left everything as though she would be back within the week.

Every day after that, Marjorie expected to hear Clem's voice on the answering machine, a little more North Country than she remembered, asking her to send on her things. It was only right, Marjorie thought. Clem's mother would need her. She could imagine how she'd feel herself if Tessa came home after all this time.

When the time did come and she heard Clem's voice on the answering machine, she decided that she would not pick up the phone. She did not want Clem being able to tell from her voice how much she missed her.

But when Clem called later that day Marjorie grabbed the receiver and they had a nice chat with no emotion in it. After that Marjorie found herself rushing to the telephone every time it rang to see if it was Clem. In between she spent much time staring out across the overgrown garden. There was snow on the ground. It was the coldest winter for fifty years. Her mind was a blank. She could see Queenie's tracks in the snow.

One day the telephone rang. It was a television producer who wanted to make something about a group of women who take the law into their own hands to get revenge on rapists. Would Marjorie act as a consultant on the production?

'It wasn't true,' she said. 'Why should I be able to help?'

'Oh, it's a drama,' the producer said. 'But after what happened you could help on what might drive a woman to do such a thing. If she did it.'

Marjorie wanted to refuse but she could not find the words to say no. She didn't know why she hadn't refused point blank. But then, of course, she told herself, I don't know why I didn't refuse to go along with any of this.

Clem rang that night. Marjorie told her about the programme. Clem tried to sound interested, but Marjorie could tell she wasn't really. She was full of news of her own. She'd heard from Constable Bill Hobbs. There was a chance he might get a transfer to the West Yorkshire police. 'I told him I'd be glad to see him,' Clem said.

'And will you?' Marjorie asked.

There was a short pause. Then Clem laughed. 'Yes,' she said. 'I will.'

'He hasn't proposed yet?' Marjorie said. Sarcasm was the only way she could deal with how happy she felt for Clem.

Marjorie hadn't expected it, but when she walked into the meeting of the television programme-makers, Fiona was there. She was pregnant but she looked rich and even more glamorous than before. The television people spoke in a horribly glib manner, Marjorie thought, and Fiona was glib too. The woman who was writing the script was a squat figure with dyed red hair. She smoked constantly and looked very intense, waving her much-bejewelled hands about as she spoke.'

'I've had a good think about it,' this woman said, 'and I think they'd have to be poor and underprivileged. It's not believable otherwise. I mean, middle class women don't do things like that. So one's a reformed junkie, she's trying to kick drugs. She's been a prostitute to feed her habit. The other is a biker girl, all black leather, tough, but she was gang-banged and she's pissed off. I haven't visualized the third one.'

She looked at Marjorie. Marjorie had the feeling she was failing the red-haired woman who, she saw now, was not young.

'I haven't visualized her yet,' the woman said, 'I think maybe she's just a menopausal loony.'

Marjorie laughed, but Fiona nodded her head and said, without a trace of irony, 'Yes, I can buy that.'

When Marjorie got home after the meeting, she made a point of watching Fiona on television. Her pretty face filled the screen. She was talking very fast, her beautiful teeth flashing as though they were part of a magician's trick. She and Bruce Wheeler sat on a settee on either side of a middle-aged woman with a long, sad face. The woman's son had stabbed and killed her violent husband while he lay in a drunken stupor. The son was now in prison.

Bruce Wheeler asked the woman, 'If your husband treated you that badly, why didn't *you* do it? You were the victim of his violence. Is it because women are intrinsically less violent than men? Is violence only a male thing?' His handsome face was grave with concern. Marjorie had seen his father's face look like that. When Tom Wheeler asked about Tessa, he'd worn that same look.

On screen, the woman ignored Bruce Wheeler.

'I don't think that's true,' Fiona said, quick as a flash. 'I think women don't behave violently because basically they know they'll get hurt if they try it. But that doesn't mean they're not violent inside, or that they wouldn't react violently if they could get away with it. Take away the physical imbalance and you'd unleash just as much violence as there is in men.'

The middle-aged mother still sat in silence. She looked beyond weeping.

Bruce Wheeler smiled at Fiona. 'You mean, Fiona, that if women banded together against a man so they were in a position of strength against him, each of them individually could be as violent as, say, a rapist is against his victim?' He thinks he's being clever, Marjorie thought. Bruce Wheeler went on, 'Would that justify 'The Furies', for instance?' he added. He's positively twinkling, Marjorie thought, and she didn't like it. She didn't like him.

On the screen the middle-aged woman seated between Fiona and Bruce Wheeler dropped her eyes. She looked as though she had fallen asleep.

'Yes, Bruce,' Fiona said, 'I think a group like 'The Furies', if they existed, would have a real function in society as a deterrent to men, which is something the law as it stands doesn't provide.'

It didn't sound to Marjorie like anything a real person would say, but there was a burst of applause from the studio audience.

Bruce Wheeler raised his eyebrows in mock alarm and this brought much laughter. 'But seriously though,' he said when the laughter stopped, 'where do you draw the line?'

He leaned across the middle-aged woman towards Fiona as he asked the question.

Marjorie thought, he's sleeping with her. I'm sure of it. Is he the father of the child? She felt sick. She suddenly wondered if Fiona hadn't had something like this in mind all along. Marjorie thought, she was after Bruce Wheeler from the start. God knows how she did it, but she's got exactly what she always wanted.

Marjorie went to turn the television off, but hesitated to press the switch. There was something fascinating about the interplay between those two.

Fiona gave a big smile. 'Well, Bruce,' she said, 'I think you'll have to ask me that question again in a few months' time. Because now I'm expecting a little baby of my own, I'm very aware that motherhood makes women feel differently about this subject. I'm sure all you mothers out there will know what

I mean.' She turned to the camera like a movie star accepting an Oscar.

Suddenly, the middle-aged woman began to weep. The camera stared in disbelief as the tears poured down her face and dripped on her blouse, leaving little dark patches. She made no noise with her tears. She sat silently weeping.

Marjorie turned off the set. She sat in front of the blank screen thinking that she was the only one alone now. Whether or not they'd really been justified in what they'd done, The Furies had brought those two to some kind of solution. But not her.

Marjorie sat back in her chair. There must be some reason to go on living, she thought. She wondered how she would go about committing suicide. She imagined herself dead in the chair with a plastic bag over her head. Someone would call the police in the end. The postman, probably, when he could no longer push the letters through the box because of the pile inside the door.

She imagined her funeral. Ben would send a wreath. No, he would come. He would have to come. It wouldn't look right if he didn't. But Peter wouldn't be there. Would Peter even bother to send flowers? It didn't matter, not any more.

She went into the kitchen and got a black

plastic bin bag out of the cupboard. It looks so harmless, she thought, but this is all you need.

She heard the phone ringing. Perhaps it was Clem. She went to hear the message.

She was startled to hear Ben's voice. She recognized him at once, of course. But he sounded like a stranger, too.

He seemed to be unsure of himself, indignant but nervous. Marjorie could imagine Nathalie standing at his shoulder, giving him no chance to weaken.

Ben said, 'Marjorie, you've got to stop dragging my name into disrepute with this dreadful publicity about that Furies business. I ask you, what are you trying to do to us?' He paused to take a breath.

Pompous idiot, Marjorie thought.

'Really, Marjorie,' he said, 'you'd think you'd have more sense at your age, getting involved in something so sordid. Nathalie says you're menopausal and you should get treatment. There is some treatment, apparently . . . '

Marjorie put out a hand to snatch up the receiver. She wanted to screech and scream at him. She wanted to tell him how he had ruined her life but she pulled her hand back. She wouldn't speak to him.

'Nathalie's even been mistaken for you at

273

the shops,' Ben was saying. 'They ask her if she's *the* Mrs Warren and what *The Furies* really did to those men. Can you imagine how she feels? And I've been asked questions at work, as if it had anything to do with me. Someone even asked me what I'd done to you to make you like that. How could you do this, Marjorie? I'm almost glad Tessa isn't here to go through what Nathalie and I are suffering because of you.'

Marjorie played the tape back, listening to the message again. Her anger evaporated as she heard his bleating voice. Instead, she felt like laughing. What a prig he was. Had he always been like that, or had Nathalie made him? No, to be fair, he'd been the same since she'd first known him; she just didn't want to see it. And here she was having wasted years torturing herself because she'd lost him. She'd thought she wasn't good enough for him. She said to herself, it's you who weren't good enough for me.

'What a fool I've been,' she said out loud.

She took the plastic bag upstairs, opened the door of Tessa's room, and, slowly and methodically, she began to throw away everything that had once been Tessa's: the hand mirror, the photographs, the junk jewellery, the shoes, the clothes, the hairbrush and curlers, still tangled with strands of golden hair. She took down the pop star posters from the wall.

She took the bulging plastic bag up the street and left it under a tree for the dustmen. She went a long way from her house because she didn't want some stray dog to break into the bag and scatter Tessa's things where she would see them from her front window.

Back in the house she played Ben's message again on the answering machine. It was really quite funny. She hoped he would call again.

Other titles published by
The House of Ulverscroft:

ASYLUM

Anthony Masters

When undercover police officer Danny Boyd accidentally kills a young asylum seeker, he is beset not only by guilt but also by his failure to get under the skin of a new identity as Rick James, ex-con with a calling to Christianity, in the rundown coastal resort of Seagate. Meanwhile, an influx of asylum seekers have replaced traditional holidaymakers in the town. As they wait for acceptance, they are also awaiting a visit from a new Balkan leader, Roma Lorta. But mayhem begins to break out. Prominent figures in the local community are murdered, and when Lorta himself is threatened, Boyd's alias takes on a new importance . . .

THE CARDAMOM CLUB

Jon Stock

Raj Nair, a young British Asian doctor, is posted to Delhi. It's his first time in India, his first job with MI6, and not everyone is pleased to see him. Ambitious and patriotic, he is soon forced to question his own loyalties, particularly when his father is arrested in Britain on spying charges. Raj realises he is up against a secretive, colonial organisation working at the very heart of Whitehall: the Cardamom Club. Is it responsible for a chilling sati and other brutalities at odds with a modern, progressive India? Can his father really be a traitor? And will Raj expose the Club before it destroys him?

SOMEWHERE, HOME

Nada Awar Jarrar

This is the story of three Lebanese women, each of them removed from home, returning to home, searching for home, for somewhere that can be home . . . Maysa returns to live in the house that belonged to her grandparents when she was a child, in a village high on Mount Lebanon, to search for her past . . . Aida returns to the Lebanon, the country of her birth, in search of the spirit of Amou Mohammed, the Palestinian refugee who was a second father to her and her sisters when she was a child . . . Salwa, now an old woman, taken by her husband from her homeland when she was a young wife and mother, recalls her life from her hospital bed, surrounded by her children and her grandson, but still, in some sense, far from home . . .

PEOPLE DIE

Kevin Wignall

JJ's a contract-killer. Working freelance for a select organisation, he's built a reputation as a discreet, professional cleaner who doesn't cause trouble for employer or 'client'. But now he's a target as well, and he doesn't know why. All he knows is that the people close to him are being killed, former allies are turning against him, and the only person offering help is the friend of one of his victims. It's one of the golden rules — never become involved with a target's friends or family, with the people who loved them. But JJ's running out of options . . .

TELEGRAM FROM THE PALACE

Geoffrey Toye

A story set against a hundred years of bloody history, from the Whitechapel Ripper murders, through the sinking of the Lusitania to the Mountbatten assassination. The ruthlessness of the IRA, the extreme violence used to combat it, and corruption in high places are further ingredients in a tangled web of intrigue . . . Lucy is dead, murdered within days of her hundredth birthday, as she had predicted to her priest. Now her killers are after her only living relative, her grandson Morgan John, who escapes to the one place where he will leave no tracks: the sea. With him aboard his ketch is journalist Deidre Gallagher, who owes John her life . . .

PAYBACK

Alan Dunn

Security consultant, ex-cop and some-time detective Billy Oliphant is suffering from more than just winter blues, and his friend, Sly, thinks that a weekend at the Forestcrag Moorland Holiday Village will cheer him up. But things there are far from idyllic; the manager believes someone is poisoning his staff. When the Village is snowed in and the body of the payroll manager is discovered, Billy reluctantly gets involved. Amongst the guests, there could be a killer. And, if the police are right that a recently escaped prisoner — a man Billy put behind bars — is heading for Forestcrag, perhaps more than one . . .